The Green Line Divide

Romance, Travel, and Turmoils

Z Vally

ISBN-10: 0993094007
ISBN-13: 978-0993094002 (Z Vally)
Library of Congress Control Number: 2014918506
Createspace Independent Publishing Platform
North Charleston, South Carolina, USA.

Published by: Z. Vally
Printed by: CreateSpace, Book ID: 4735516,
4900 LaCross Road, North Charleston, South Carolina 29406, USA
To contact: zvallyauthor@gmail.com

About the Author

In the 1980s, Z. Vally lived in Cyprus near the Green Line (buffer zone). She enjoyed living there. She travelled to Rhodes Island, Greece, on a cruise liner, *Princess Marissa*, which does not exist now. She now lives in the United Kingdom. She studied business and finance at a British college.

Cyprus has been mentioned as it stands in reality. The demarcation line is supervised by the United Nations after the Turkish invasion in 1974. Readers who are not familiar with the geography of Cyprus should note the following:

- Greek-speaking side of the Republic of Cyprus, in the south of Cyprus
- Turkish speaking side, or Turkish occupied side, in the north of Cyprus, under the control of the Turkish occupied troops.

The author has no political interest in Cyprus. She is neither Cypriot nor Turkish.

The tales surrounding the buffer zone are fictitious, as are some of the other tales. But some of the narratives are true. The towns, villages, sites, and beverages are real.

The Green Line Divide

Romance, Travel, and Turmoils

Z. Vally

Thanks to the special **One** *who gave me
the wonderful gift of writing,
and
to all who provided me with the information for
this book. They are too many to mention here.*

Contents

SKETCH OF CYPRUS

Morphou Bay

NORTH

Nicosia

Famagusta

Ayia Napa

Larnaca

SOUTH

Troodos

P

K

O

Limassol

Akrotiri Bay

Paphos

Akrotiri UK Base

K = Kakopetria
P = Platres
O = Omodos

▲ = Mt Olympus
D = Dhekelia UK Base

SKETCH OF RHODES ISLAND, GREECE

ANO
SYMI
ISLAND

RHODES
MH
Kos
K
F
T A
V
Af
Anthony
Quinn Bay
S
Km
NISSOS
CHALKI
Em
Ar
Ts
Lindos
St Pauls
Bay

Cape Prasonisi

MH = Mandraki
        Harbour
Kos = Koskinou
K = Kalithea
A = Ammoudes
F = Faliraki
Af = Afandou
Km = Kolymbia
Ar = Archangelos
Ts = Tsambika
        Beach
L = Lalysos
P = Paradisi
T = Theologou
V = Valley of
        Butterflies
Em = Embona
S = Seven Springs

Prologue

Nicosia, Cyprus, 1983

The plane was slowly descending in altitude. Below, Alexis glimpsed a mass of blue sea and an area of land with rooftops and rectangular fields. A sharp announcement in a Greek accent aired from the loudspeakers across the cabin.

"We are reaching Larnaca International Airport. Get your belongings ready."

Larnaca is the third largest town in Cyprus, situated on the southern coast. It is a seaside town with long stretches of sandy beaches, a port, and the island's largest airport. It is known for its palm tree seafront. Its tourist attractions feature the ancient churches, a mosque, a fort, and a salt lake visited by pink flamingos.

This was not the first time Alexis had been to Cyprus. She had been here before to see her grandparents, who lived in a village outside Nicosia. But she had asked the college to arrange to pick her up and transport her to her accommodations. She hadn't wanted to bother her grandparents; they would have had to travel a good distance and had a commitment to their farm.

A wave of shuffling noises emerged as passengers got ready to disembark. Children became excited, as some were on holiday; Cyprus was a popular destination for British tourists. The passengers were pulling sun hats, coloured sunglasses, and sun cream out of their luggage cabin bags and hurriedly rubbing the cream on their arms and legs. They were joyous and emitted smiled at the sight of the little ones.

Alexis came down the plane stairway carrying her hand luggage. She looked sporty in her khaki Bermuda shorts, yellow cotton top, khaki baseball cap, and brown sandals. Her hair was neat in a ponytail. She queued for the passport control under the British queue sign and glided across the barriers due to her Cypriot blood connections.

Cypriots were patriotic, and Cyprus was comprised of Greek Cypriots, Turkish Cypriots, Armenians, Maronites, and Latins. It was a British colony until 1960, when it became independent from Britain and became a republic.

Alexis collected her luggage, put on her sunglasses, and headed outside into the hot sunshine. The college had promised a taxi man would be outside holding a sign with her college name on it. But instead, she saw her name, "Alexis T.," printed on a rectangular poster. She gave a sigh of relief; at least someone had come to pick her up.

She walked towards the placard and said that she was Alexis Theodorou. The stout taxi man shook her hand, cheerfully took her luggage, and motioned to a waiting red Jaguar. She was bemused but decided not to question the mode of transportation. She felt that Cyprus was safe.

The taxi man opened the back door for her. "How was your journey?"

"Good," Alexis replied courteously.

He placed her luggage in the boot with a smile on his face. He drove off, leaning across to switch on the radio, filling the air with Greek music.

Alexis comfortably sat in the backseat. She stretched her legs and watched the dry, arid scenery go by. It was the end of August, and the harsh midafternoon sun beamed in her face. She was enjoying the sunrays as well as the stylish ride in the air-conditioned car with soft leather seats.

After thirty-five minutes, they reached Nicosia. The car turned uphill into a grand entrance of what appeared to be a five-star hotel, Blue Ballantyne. The square building had blue stained-glass windows and blue exterior walls. Blue columns at its four corners had lamps that no doubt lit the night with blue lighting. This cool-looking blue gem sat elegantly on the flattened top of a hill, like a sapphire on a lady's headband, accompanied by a flowing blue chiffon gown.

Alexis squinted her eyes with curiosity. *What is going on?* The taxi driver drove up to the entrance and stopped.

"Your destination, madam," he said.

"Oh, here?" she asked, puzzled.

The porter came, collected her luggage, and asked her to follow him. She went to the reception desk, gave her name, and collected the keys.

Her suite was on the sixth floor, which had a taste of opulence. It looked like a floor reserved for celebrities.

Hmmm…a student accommodation, here? she pondered. *Perhaps this is the way students are welcomed.*

Her thoughts were interrupted by the polite voice of a female staff member of the hotel, who had joined the porter.

"Madam, do you want your meal delivered to your room, or will you go downstairs to the dining room?"

"I'll go downstairs, thank you," Alexis responded.

"Meal will be in one and a half hours' time," the woman added.

The woman and the porter left Alexis to settle in.

Alexis set the travel alarm clock, removed her baseball cap, and drifted off to sleep. The sharp ringing of the alarm clock woke her up some time later. She refreshed herself and went downstairs for dinner in the same clothes.

She found her corner table and was joined by a respectable-looking, high-ranking army officer on his way home to Sweden, who told her about the United Nations peacekeeping force in Cyprus. She told him that she was a student, and he in return informed her that he was going home to attend his daughter's college graduation. He suggested in passing that Alexis might like going to Olynasa Pub, in downtown Nicosia, where his peacekeeping officers often gathered for a drink. Alexis widened her eyes with glee and took an earnest note of the officer's recommendation in her handbook. He finished his meal and left her to finish hers.

Alexis had a hearty three-course meal, buffet style. She picked up a blue ocean-print tray and selected a healthy choice of fresh watermelon, Greek salad, and Mediterranean fish stew with garlic bread. An aroma of parsley and cooked white wine lingered, accompanied by a cocktail of pomegranate juice: a lemony taste with a dash of vodka. And she took her time over it; light music was playing in the background. Later, she topped off her dinner with a local honey cheesecake, flavoured with orange and rose water, topped with pistachios and almonds.

When she finished, she went upstairs via a lift purposely scented by the cleaning staff. The lift doors opened on the sixth floor, and outside her door was a distinguished lady puffing on a cigarette with a sea of suitcases. Amid the tobacco smoke, a strong scent of expensive perfume filtered through the air, which compensated for the chimney smoke coming from the cigarette. Her hair was covered in a white bandana that matched her halter-neck dress. A member of the hotel staff, who seemed to be her personal assistant, stood next to her.

The lady was furious! She was like a lioness that had witnessed her cubs being disturbed.

"Elena, tell her that she is in the wrong room!" the angry lady howled. Flinging her free hand in the air, she said, "She must vacate the room immediately."

Alexis was bewildered. It was also nighttime; the college was closed. Where could she go now?

The personal assistant took Alexis aside and calmly explained the situation to her. Alexis's taxi driver was waiting for her downstairs to take her to *her* hotel. There had been a mix-up at the airport, as her big-wheel boss was also Alexis T.! She was the singer, Alexis Theodorou. She had the same name!

Alexis gave a controlled giggle and turned to look at the lioness glaring at her. At this moment, she thought of the ordinary taxi the celebrity had probably been driven in, which probably did not have air conditioning. She wanted to laugh aloud, but she did not dare to do so. Instead, she apologised and opened the door. She called for the porter on the intercom system to help her with her one suitcase. Alexis collected her hand luggage and swiftly made for the lift, where she was met by the reluctant-looking female staff member who had attended her previously. She had come to sort out the paperwork. She smiled at Alexis and wished her well.

Her taxi driver was apologetic and began to drive down the hill.

"Oh, not to worry," Alexis said. "I had a taste of high society life."

They both burst out laughing.

Alexis T. was a singer on a tour who sang in multiple languages. She was due to perform at the stadium in Nicosia. The taxi driver had first taken the singer to Alexis's three-star hotel, Hotel Saffron, and he had had to make a quick U-turn to the prestigious hotel where the singer had booked a suite. She was seething! At this point, the taxi man was unaware of her status. A van followed them with the singer's pile of luggage, arranged at the airport by the personal assistant. His four-door car was not going to be enough, even if it was turned into a trailer!

Alexis spent a week at Hotel Saffron before being transferred to a student hostel. During that week, Alexis visited her grandparents and saw how strong they both still were, mentally and physically. Alexis figured it was due to all the olive oil.

The singer Alexis T. performed at the GSP Stadium in Nicosia, and Grandma Cordelia and her husband, Pierre, were in the audience.

College began in mid-September, and Alexis spent three years studying until the time came for her final exams.

Hard work produces results. It can be accomplished if one is determined and strives for it.

Three Years Later

Chapter 1

Summer of 1986

It was a beautiful, warm summer's day in August 1986, on an island off the southern part of Cyprus. Alexis walked out of a building on the Burling College campus with the result of her exam in business studies. She had failed the exam. Burling College was British. All she thought of now was how she was going to resit the exams and how she would acquire the funding for it. She became anxious and mulled it over for some days. She had studied hard, but to pass, she had to pass all four subjects in financial accounts, auditing and taxation, cost accounts, and computer technology together. She went down in accounts, which gave her the overall failing mark.

Some days later, as she waited for a bus during these worrying days, she saw some girls in uniform coming out of a hotel. She had a "eureka" moment. She had a constructive idea, and bright sparks went through her head. She would put an advertisement in the English-speaking newspaper *Destiny Weekly* announcing her availability to do housekeeping and babysitting jobs for private households. The publication date was set for the coming Friday.

At the newspaper's office was a male receptionist. He was in his fifties and had an average build, shoulder-length, thin, straight black hair, and a black moustache. He wore thick, black, square-framed glasses. His job was to take the advertisements. He repeatedly glanced at her and then at the paper he was writing on. His upper lip twitched, which made his moustache tremor. He furrowed his brow and looked at her questioningly. Alexis grew nervous and giggled, chewing bubble gum to overcome her nerves.

She said in a funny tone, "Alexis is my name, which means helper, and I can be that helping mermaid who can swim to the deep end to get the job done." She chewed on her gum rapidly.

"Mmmm," came the shallow response from the receptionist.

Alexis paid for the advertisement, and as she left, she twitched her eyebrows and widened her eyes at this man behind the desk, creating a funny face. She had grown bored of his seriousness.

This man at last laughed and told her in a sarcastic tone, "Good luck, and come back again for more ads. My name is Leon."

"Thank you, Mr. Leon. I am sure I will be back," she replied, smiling. She blew a big pink bubble with her gum, out of mischief. She then pouted, as if she were bored.

As Alexis was leaving, she looked into the depth of his office and saw that it was messy. She asked him if he needed his headquarters to be cleaned or organised. He returned an abrasive, rapid no and buried his head back into the paper pad he was writing on.

Alexis Theodorou was twenty-four years old, and she spoke fluent English, as she had grown up in England. She spoke Greek, but she was not so eloquent in it. She was a good-looking, feisty, and witty brunette of medium height. She had brown coloured Anglo-Greek eyes that were slightly almond shaped under two well-shaped eyebrows. Her sharp, tilted nose had an Anglo touch, and a canopy of long, straight, chestnut-brown hair covered her head.

A red bucket hat shielded her face from the sun, and she wore a red scarf with a print on it of a yellow flower on a stalk. When she rode her bicycle, she wore sunglasses and cycled with care.

On the highway, the distance of the road deceived her. Her cycling journey on this still, hot, sunny day seemed never to end. A heat shimmer created an image of a pool of water on the road. The optical illusion kept on moving, frustrating her journey.

Alexis waited impatiently for Friday, when the advertisement would come out. Work would be limited at this time of the year because many were still on holiday, and it was still early for Christmas cleaning. Then, at nightfall, a call came through as Alexis was getting ready for bed.

"Room number one, your phone," she heard a man call out loudly outside her door. Alexis jumped as if it was a call for a fire evacuation. She went to the phone.

"Hello, I am from room one. Can I help you, please?" Alexis asked triumphantly.

A lady replied, "We read your advertisement, and we would like to know what you charge for babysitting."

"Oh…" Alexis stammered. It was silly of her not to have thought of the prices. Without thinking, she quoted three Cyprus pounds per hour.

"Thank you. We will call you back," was the reply.

Alexis realised that she had to research the price.

The following day, she went to Dionys Supermarket and asked the proprietor's wife for prices for different types of household duties. The husband and wife ran the supermarket as a jolly team. The husband found it very amusing that Alexis, the bicycle girl, was going to get someone's house in shipshape. He laughed and joked that a man might spring from his blankets as she walked in to make his bed!

When Alexis returned that afternoon to her room, she had a message for her to call a number back, which she did. A gentleman picked up the phone. He spoke in a Greek accent. He asked her to meet him that night at eight o'clock behind the Trixos Building. He told her where the building was. Alexis found this arrangement scary, but he said he was a family man and needed someone to make their house sparkle. The request seemed genuine.

He was about to put the phone down when Alexis called out, "But wait. I don't know your name, and how will I recognise you?" He gave his name as George, and the colour of his car was dark blue. He also asked Alexis to bring her passport. She told him that he would recognise her from her red bicycle.

"Bicycle!" he exclaimed.

3

"Yes," Alexis replied. She almost giggled. Did he expect her to come in a Mercedes-Benz? She could not understand why he found it odd to be using a bicycle when it was common on the island for foreign girls to ride them. He must have been an oddball or a very busy man not to have seen this. Alarm bells began to ring, but she needed the money to complete her studies.

It was a cool summer day. On arrival, she noticed the dark blue car. He called out for her to come to his car. It was a small Mercedes. Alexis parked her bicycle on its stand and went to join him. The only light came from the flats surrounding the building. Alexis had an eerie feeling about this meeting. She opened the door and kept one leg outside with the door open. She could vaguely see his face but could see a silhouette of a man with a large build. After saying hello, she quickly showed him her British passport. He would have certainly needed light to scrutinise her identification, but instead of switching on the overhead car light, he pulled out a torch and shone it on the passport. Alexis thought he would soon turn it on her face, and she had prepared herself to make a clown face if he did that. She wore white Bermuda shorts and a green T-shirt. Without her red bucket hat, her funny face would have beamed in full view under the flashing light. It did not look as if he was interested in her face but was very likely aiming more for her bare legs, which were slim and strong from cycling.

George was a tall, slim, presentable man in his early forties. He had a Greek accent. He said he had previously lived abroad for a while but left because of street crime. That type of crime was unheard of on this side of Cyprus; it was very safe. His outward appearance made him seem believable. Alexis was streetwise, though. She was astute and observant—not gullible.

To avoid further intrusive questions, she quickly told him that she was Anglo-Greek and spoke little Greek. Her father was Greek Cypriot, and her mother was English, but she did not see a purpose in revealing all of this, so she kept quiet. She did not like talking about herself. Surprisingly, George did not ask for the reason she wanted this job. Did he have another interest? He looked at her from head to toe. As far as Alexis could gather, this had nothing to do with domestic work. Alexis looked sideways. She wanted him to know that she had no interest in him other than a respectable job.

"Age?" he asked.

She cut him short and said in a hurried tone, "Twenty-four."

He went back to her passport for the date of birth and began to count on his fingers. Alexis wished a calculator would drop from the sky into his lap to help him compute the age.

This whole interview was getting quite annoying. He gave her back her passport and smiled at her, as if she had won his approval.

"Shall we go to my office?" he asked, and he pointed to a block of flats.

Alexis glared at him. This man just needed two tusks, which would make him look like an elephant!

"What for?" Alexis retorted. She could not hold back the pain of the humiliation anymore. For the time she had wasted, she could have utilised it studying for her exams.

"I am only interested in a cleaning job and not giving you a clean-up job!" she said angrily.

She pulled her passport from his hands and left the car. Infuriated, she mounted her bicycle and rode in a rage towards her bedsit. The night wind blowing in her face helped soothe her anger. When she reached her room, she thought about what had happened. She should have expected this from a man who had asked her to meet him behind a building. *At least he was civilised enough not to have forced anything upon me. I will have to be more cautious next time, though,* came to her as words of wisdom. Alexis felt more safe and carefree here in Cyprus than in England, though.

What was this man's problem that he had to go to this great length to chat up a lady? Surely, there were plenty of women around for a man of his status.

But she never got an answer for this.

Alexis's room was a comfortable one, with all the requirements necessary for a student, but could she find peace of mind in this place at night? No, the other students in the building slept through the hot Mediterranean afternoon and stayed awake through the cooler nights! From right above her room, she could hear young men from the Middle East talking and laughing loudly with music from the stereo blaring, without any consideration of others around them. As if this was not enough, they were beating the drums too. Alexis felt as if the floor above her was about to crack onto her head. All varieties of music were present in that room, except for the police siren!

She went upstairs to ask them to lower their music, but they slammed the door in her face. They were not prepared to listen, and Alexis went for a long bicycle ride to calm her mind. The cool air blowing in her face was always a welcoming sensation to refresh her mind. She came back to find the boys from upstairs had left, and it was quiet. But she knew she would have to leave the student hostel if she wanted to pass her exams. She ate, refreshed herself, and sat down to study. It was late, but this was the best time, as it was cool too.

An American missionary family came to Alexis's aid. Mrs. Janice Williams, a friendly, soft-spoken woman with four children, gave Alexis a housecleaning job on an irregular basis. At least the job started Alexis off. Alexis began to learn from Mrs. Williams and enjoyed working for her. She had a colourful house on the upper floor of a two-story building. An ambience of Christianity filled the air. Wooden templates of biblical scriptures hung in every room, and potted green plants gave a touch of the Garden of Eden. Alexis always had a beautiful feeling being in that house.

Mrs. Williams never overworked her, and before she left her house, she always asked Alexis what lunch she would like to have. She went for an omelette so as not to bother her with the preparation. Alexis looked forward to all sorts of different fillings. She also provided her with a hearty coffee break of homemade cookies; Mrs. Williams took care of her well-being.

She was a calm, simple lady of European descent, with a tall physique, short black hair, and flat kneecaps. She dressed in frocks and wore matching flat shoes. Her dresses had wide pockets in the front, and inside them, she kept her list of daily chores, which she had to consult from time to time, as she talked to it, to remind her. The shoes had to be flat, as she had to do a lot of running around the spacious flat, especially when the children were around. They ran from room to room, as they did not have a garden to play in; they lived in the upstairs section of the massive house. Well, a domestic help was certainly a relief for Mrs. Williams.

Cyprus and Nicosia

The island of Cyprus in the Mediterranean Sea was invaded in July 1974. Half of Cyprus, the northern and eastern parts, had been occupied by Turkey, where the Turkish-speaking Cypriots moved, and the southern part of Cyprus was left for the Greek-speaking Cypriots. This was the reason for the presence of the peacekeeping forces (United Nations) in Nicosia and other areas; they looked after the dividing line that created a buffer zone between the north and south of Cyprus.

Nicosia was a divided capital city (at this time, it was similar to East and West Berlin, Germany). In the south was the Greek speaking side of the city, and the north was a self-proclaimed Turkish occupied side. It was the capital city of Cyprus on both sides. The dividing buffer zone was known as the Green Line, after the green pen colour used by a United Nations officer to draw the line on the map of the city. Barbed wire and tower guards divided the no-man's-land, and one could go from one side to the other using a passport. But access to the locals from both sides was not allowed; only foreigners were permitted. There were two checkpoint gates in Nicosia to use, to go from one side to the other. These were Ledra Street and Ledra Palace crossings, for pedestrian tourists only, and were manned by the United Nations force to keep the two warring sides separate.

The United Nations officers who came into Nicosia town centre were mainly from Scandinavia, Canada, and, sometimes, the Great Britain force. They headed for the pubs. Alexis had a younger student friend, Molly, and she would spend her free time from her studies min-gling with the officers. Alexis would join in on some days. The girls got to know two particular pubs in the old part of Nicosia that the United Nations forces mainly went to, and these were within a short distance of each other. So, Molly and Alexis ran "errands" from one to another, weaving among the Filipino girls who worked in the nightclubs, hop-ing that Molly and Alexis would get attention from the United Nations officers. They sure did, as they had the ability to have flowing conversa-tions in English. Some officers were kind and bought drinks for these poor misers only because Molly cheered them up; Alexis remained in the shadows.

Molly was a young African girl in a senior private school. Over the summer holidays, she worked as a live-in governess for a wealthy Greek family. The family had a soft spot for her and cared for her, and she enjoyed working for them. Molly was streetwise and very mature for her age. She made people laugh and was funny with the children too. She was good fun to be around, so everybody liked her.

The old city of Nicosia on the Greek speaking side was dotted with museums, ancient churches, and medieval buildings, and it offered the Hamam Turkish baths and the Watchtower on the Green Line. The majority who visited the baths were men who came to refresh their busi-ness minds and to keep their physical bodies healthy; middle-aged, pot-bellied men were a common sight here. From the Watchtower, one could view the north of Nicosia, and what a contrasting image it gave. Nicosia was more bustling with activity in the south than the Turkish occupied side, which was more sombre with its abandoned buildings. But the Selimiye Mosque in the north dominated the city's skyline, even from the Green Line. It had been a cathedral before and now had become a tourist attraction for its Gothic architecture.

The old city of Nicosia was within a circular wall in the shape of a flower. Alexis at a later stage would come to live near the historic Ledra Street, which is in the middle of the old city of Nicosia. The old city led to narrow streets with dusty boutiques, artist's cafés, guesthouses, jewellery shops, and bicycle repair shops where Alexis got her bicycle mended. Small stores or workshops occupied the bottom floors of the city's buildings, and above were the houses where people talked to each other across the slim road. It created a noisy and informal atmosphere.

On the Greek speaking side, a square linked the old city to the new cosmopolitan city of Nicosia. It was becoming a modern business and cultural centre, with European-flavoured, cosmopolitan stores. The development was moving fast. Roads and attractive Mediterranean-style houses were being built. It displayed progress and wealth.

Alexis, being British-born, held a neutral view on this conflict. She counted herself as a semiforeigner; her grandparents from her father's side thought of her as zany.

Chapter 2

Molly and Ayia Napa

The most unwanted news came. Molly was leaving the island sometime in the year. She was going back home to be with her family. She was the last of the foreign friends Alexis had still remaining on this island. Alexis felt down about Molly's departure. Molly had plans to go for a hitchhike spree to a seaside town; she had been known to hitchhike from one seaside town to another in one night. It was safe. If she got bored in a disco in Limassol, she would head to the streets, sticking her thumb out, heading to Ayia Napa. She had a loveable chubby look about her, with her bulging teenage tummy sticking out. She was not pregnant but looked it. She would stand there smiling, showing her protruding white teeth, which stood out well against her skin colour, her Afro hair brushed neatly upwards, looking like spikes. She wore shorts and a T-shirt, which did not fully cover her bulging teenage stomach, and oval, black-framed eyeglasses sliding down her nose. She was nothing fashionable compared with the other people in the disco! She displayed an innocence that went with her age, and it seemed men felt sorry for her. And being black attracted more attention, as it was unusual to see a black face on the island. Someone always stopped to give her a lift; the kind ones probably felt sorry for her. She had plenty of laughable stories of her hitchhiking adventures. Molly wanted Alexis to have a hitchhiking experience with her.

"You are not going to solve your problems by remaining in your bedsit," she said. She added with a firm tone, "These noisemakers living above you will always be around whether you are in or out."

Alexis had gotten into the habit of staying in her bedsit to take advantage of the quiet times to study when she was not working. She would wait for Molly to come and tell her funny stories to cheer her up. Alexis enjoyed Molly's company, as she made her laugh.

Alexis felt Molly was right, and she agreed to go with her. Molly was going to introduce Alexis to hitchhiking! Molly was out to change her and show Alexis her world. They decided to start off late in the afternoon for the seaside town of Ayia Napa, so they would be in time to go straight to the disco instead of queuing outside, waiting for it to open.

Ayia Napa was a place created for tourists, and women were allowed to walk about topless on the beach. All shapes and sizes, from meringues to papayas, were on free display! It was a clubbing seaside town, and a place for relationships if you were looking for one. Ironically, Ayia in Greek meant *holy*, but there was no sign of holiness here! And Napa meant *wooded valley*, as it was one, before some areas were flattened to make it into a tourist attraction. Ayia Napa was a busy resort situated on the south of Famagusta, on the southern coast of Cyprus, the far eastern side. It attracted tourists for its long stretches of sandy beaches and water sports. It was a favourite spot for British and Scandinavian tourists.

Alexis and Molly set off for Ayia Napa with their rucksacks on their backs. Alexis watched Molly hitchhike, giggling as she handled the job of finding a lift for them. Molly confidently stood on the left side of the road, as it was left-hand driving in Cyprus, sticking her thumb out to motion for a lift. Alexis was afraid of being recognised by someone from the college or a Greek relative, so she wore a straight golden-brown wig, which glistened down below her shoulder and had a thick hair fringe floating over her forehead. If a car did not stop, Molly would say funny remarks about the driver and shout after them, "Your tyres would go flat with us inside, hey?" or "Your car is too posh for us," making the driver's head turn towards them, and perhaps he or she would be glad

11

not to have stopped. Alexis was beginning to enjoy the thrills from this escapade. It was a short-term medicine for her exam worries.

At last, one car stopped for them. The driver agreed to take them to a junction near their destination. The hitchhiking journey went by with the usual questions. Molly knew what the next answer would be before the question was asked! She was experienced with conversations while hitchhiking. They got halfway and got off at a crossroad to Ayia Napa. Their subsequent lift was in a dark maroon Range Rover.

Alexis pushed Molly into the front, and she went off to the backseat. Alexis was not acquainted with conversing while hitchhiking. In the back was space for her legs and her rucksack, which she removed from her back. She began to feel comfortable. The usual script began to flow in the front, which had become boring and routine for Molly. She wanted excitement and to get to the disco quickly.

"What is your name?" the driver asked Molly.

"Diana Ross." Molly jumped in quickly to answer in a calm, grown-up tone.

Alexis shot up from her slouching posture, as she was about to doze off at the back. She couldn't believe her ears. Molly was black, but she definitely could not pass herself off for a well-known singer! Molly was a chubby girl of medium height and did not look anywhere close to the singer. Laughter wanted to burst from Alexis's mouth, but she managed to control it forcefully, whereas Molly just smiled sarcastically. This was nothing new to her.

The driver paused as he looked at her questioningly. He was no fool. He was a schoolteacher, and he jolly well knew who Diana Ross was. The British singer certainly would not be getting a lift from him!

"What about your friend in back?" he continued to probe.

Alexis buried her face in her rucksack, not knowing what to expect from Molly.

"Oh, she is Barbara Streisand," she informed him innocently, without even giggling.

That did it for the driver. He began to pull her hair in a joking manner. He undid the ribbon from her hair and poked her arm lightly.

"Stop it!" shouted Molly, moving away from the driver's seat. She felt like a trapped animal in a cage in the front seat.

Alexis was bursting with laughter, and she knew he was not trying to harm her. It was his way to have fun too! Alexis wanted to be mischievous too and wanted to hit the driver jokingly from the back with her bag but decided not to, as he could stop the car and ask them to get out, which she did not want. The "poking" continued until they reached the second turnoff to Ayia Napa. It was nighttime now, and they needed another lift to take them from the crossroad to the clubbing seaside town.

They got one. They told the van driver they were going to Ayia Napa. The farmer huddled them in the front of the heavily loaded van, and he asked them the usual question of what they were doing in Cyprus.

"We are both students," Alexis answered. Being seated next to the driver, she decided to take the lead.

"And we are going to the disco," she said to cut his questionings short, as they were tired of answering the same questions. The driver was too fatigued to query them further and drove slowly because of the load, but the sluggish ride put Molly to sleep.

When they reached Ayia Napa, which looked like a long ride, the driver stopped and hooted loudly to wake Molly up. At the same time, Alexis nudged her too. Molly shuddered from her sleep, and the driver snuffled a laugh.

"Are we in Ayia Napa?" Molly asked, half-asleep.

"Yes, we are. Let's go," replied Alexis. She was wide-awake because she was used to staying awake at night for her studies.

Molly shot up at Alexis's answer. Both picked up their rucksacks from their feet, thanked the driver in Greek, and made their journey to the town square, which was in the town centre. From here, they would choose a disco, as there were quite a few in the vicinity of the square. Right next to the cobbled and clubbing square was a Venetian-age monastery. And this made them giggle, as they saw the humorous side of the two differing neighbours!

On the way to the square, Molly brought up the pinches from the previous driver and strongly suggested that thereafter Alexis should sit in the front seat. The square was filled with people queuing to go into the discos. Some were coming in and out of the discos with drinks in their hands. Molly jumped the queue, and, surprisingly, nobody stopped her. At the entrance door, she was pleased to find a doorman she knew. Alexis followed her shepherd like a timid lamb. She gave him a sympathetic look with a show of her white teeth, and he let her in free. As the doorman turned his attention to the next client, she dragged Alexis with her hand, and Alexis got tugged in free too. Molly knew the ropes! That next client was a Swedish peacekeeping officer in his civilian clothes. When he got in with his ticket, he waved his forefinger laughingly at the girls who got in free and shook his head at their adventure. He got chatting and dancing with Alexis. His name was Sven Karlsson, and he later moved on to dance with a blond girl who outwardly looked more dazzling than Alexis, and who would cause a stir for him down the line.

They spent a joyous night at the disco, dancing away, joining in the crowd and keeping an eye on their rucksacks. Alexis paid for her drinks, but guess how Molly received hers? It was laughter that paid the bills for her! She created a free bills avenue.

Around three in the morning, they began to feel sleepy, and they went looking on the streets, lined with houses, for an open-front veranda. They found one. The house was small, simple, and not gated, and it had an open-front veranda.

Alexis and Molly settled down on the stone porch floor on their bath towels. It was very quiet, and they had to suppress their giggles. It was a warm night, but being an island, the land received chilly air from the sea. It tended to get cold as the night lingered on, and they had to be prepared to cover up. But morning was not far away, and the breakfast would be such a sight for the owners! Molly did not have a care for her tomorrow, and she slept soundly. Alexis, on the other hand was nervous, since it was her first experience being in Ayia Napa, and sleeping on a stranger's veranda, so she slept lightly.

After three hours into morning, a cock crowed from a nearby home, followed by footsteps. The air was crisp. Molly quickly reached for her eyeglasses. Near her were the two large feet of the owner of the house! Molly looked a sight with her Afro spiked up. The owner was a stocky man in shorts and sandals, fuming and cursing in Greek. Molly tried to give him her trademark sympathetic look by smiling and showing her white teeth, miming for mercy. But he was like an eagle ready to swoop on his prey mercilessly. He looked at Alexis, who was up and packing up her belongings, and he sent his sandals flying at her. Still angry, he went to break a branch from a nearby orange tree from his garden. The girls knew they were in trouble now!

"Out you go," he shouted at them, waving his branch at them, cursing every now and again. He shooed them off with his waving branch as if they were poultry on his porch. His hands were flying in all directions, brandishing the branch.

The girls by now had packed up in fear of this stout man. They darted out, whimpering a sorry, and ducked under and evaded the erratic swinging branch. They made a beeline for the open entrance. Would they ever choose this veranda again? No! Nobody would or should. They were scared. This was not a monastery! No compassion here, as they had been hoping for.

As soon as they reached the street safely, they looked at each other and burst out laughing. They looked back at the raging man on the porch, and he had his one hand held upwards in the air with the branch as if to warn them that he had no empathy for them if they dare return. This was Molly's method of a seaside livelihood; it was short-term fun.

They headed for the beach. It was quiet, and some were out already for an early sun. They were hungry and bought a pitta sandwich from a nearby seaside café that was getting ready to open up. They had a swim and went to sleep on the beach to overcome their drowsiness. They appreciated that they did not have to pay to use the beach. If they did, they would have found a way to use this free too!

Late afternoon, they were back on the road, looking for a lift. This time, Molly forced Alexis to stick her thumb out for a lift, and a taxi stopped.

"No money," they told the driver straight-faced, keeping their fun side under control. The driver knew they were silly girls. He was used to foreign girls' mischievous tactics. He gave in to their plea.

"Where to?" asked the driver.

"Nicosia," came a reply from Alexis. He made a quick hand-waving gesture, asking them to get in swiftly, as if he were directing the sheep into a pen! The taxi was going in that direction anyway, and he had no selfish desire to drive an empty taxi back to Nicosia. The two giggling girls got in hurriedly before the driver changed his mind, and Molly surely kept to her word and pushed Alexis to sit in the front. The taxi driver asked the usual preliminary questions, and after Alexis answered him in a tired and bored tone, he decided to leave her alone. She was too pleased with the new mute arrangement. She instead began to enjoy the passing tranquil view of the vineyards, olive trees, fruit orchards, potato farms, and grazing livestock. This was what city dwellers did not often get to see. It was a welcome break for Alexis's mind, which was accustomed to the cramped hostel's concrete structure and its surroundings.

They got a straight lift to Nicosia and were dropped on the side of the main road. From there they walked to the student hostel to have a long rest, but being able to do so was questionable. It was time for Alexis to move from here now that Molly was leaving. She placed this thought on her priority list.

Chapter 3

Army Saga and Job Trials

Alexis had her Mondays off, but on Tuesdays she worked with Mrs. Williams. She was always able to fit her in, as she did not have much work. The advertisement had not gone over too well. She was hoping to fill up more days, as her studies required revision only. She needed to get serious now about work, as she needed to pay for her exams and living expenses.

Alexis had other hobbies too. She was very keen on the distinct architecture of the Mediterranean houses. They were usually not higher than two storeys. They had large windows and exteriors in white, cream, or a sunny neutral colour. They had shallow, sloping roofs covered with roof tiles in bright terracotta. The roofs jutted out from the walls to provide extra shade for the balconies or verandas.

New houses were being built on the outskirts of the cities. The island was expanding, and fast too. Alexis found that some houses were quite attractive and had a cheerful appeal. She would get off her bicycle in Nicosia and take pictures of these residences with her camera.

One day, however, the Greek Cypriot army police stopped her. They took the camera away from her and led her to a nearby army office. Alexis realised that the reason they had stopped her was because she was in the locality of an army camp. The officers firmly interrogated her in English. They asked what she was doing in Cyprus and why she was taking pictures in this particular area. She responded to their queries. She was not scared of being questioned; this was not a dictatorship government, and she had nothing to hide. Alexis was slightly frightened, though, that she might not see her camera again. The officers had confiscated her camera because they wanted to know what other pictures she had taken and to see from the photos if she was operating as a spy. She was not, and so she had nothing to worry about. She was dismissed without her camera. After leaving the army camp, Alexis felt slightly shaken up.

After some days, her camera was returned to her home address with developed photos and the original negatives. She gave a sigh of relief and gained confidence in the governing structure of the country. One photo got her attention, and she laughed at the picture, which was of a disused car that had a large car rack that was used as a chicken coop! The car had no tyres or windows, and the chickens were free to run in and out of the car and to climb or fly to the top of the car. Alexis, for a moment, wished she could be that chicken, free from any concern in this world, including the plate it would end up on!

Alexis also got another irregular job from the advertisement. It was with an elderly man with a slight hunchback, who read his newspapers at night, as he received them late. He was Mr. Sophoclis, a Greek Orthodox from across the Mediterranean Sea, from the conflicting zone of the middle east. There is a large population of Greek Orthodox still living in that region. He had rough facial skin, which looked like eroded sand dunes, and a thin hairline that was barely hanging on. He was a divorced man who seemed bitter about it. He lived in a neglected apartment with only the basic necessities. He was on a tight budget, and fortunately he did not have to visit a barber due to sparse hair on his head. The environment was cold. He kept a good eye on Alexis and timed her chores closely. All this just amused her. The only time he left her alone was when she had to use the washroom, which had no windows. When she came out, she would find him pacing up and down the passageway. He would immediately go in after her to tour his musty bathroom and check that all was still in place and that Alexis had not pocketed his small slab of soap or the toilet roll! Alexis could not give his home a proper freshening due to the lack of quality detergents. She asked him to get better cleaning products for her to use. He never did.

Mr. Sophoclis worked from home as a journalist and translator, as he spoke Greek, Arabic, and Hebrew. When Alexis's work was over, she was too glad to get away from there with her day's wage and a packaged supermarket sandwich in her hand. She did not like eating there. He gave her a snack only because it was part of the job agreement. Alexis insisted on it.

Samee

Alexis placed another advertisement in the same newspaper, which brought a smile to Mr. Leon's drooping face. The island had a constant flow of English-speaking foreigners coming and leaving, so Alexis hoped new arrivals would read her advertisement. Her snag was that she did not have a private phone in her room, and the only phone access was a communal coin-box in the hostel. She could only give out this phone number for the newspaper.

A phone call came through, and since the phone box was near her room, she picked it up. It was a young-sounding, professional voice with an Arabic accent. He called himself Samee. He said they needed an au pair for three days a week, which Alexis said she could do. Alexis went through the usual introductory questions and answers. He agreed to her working conditions. She was invited for an interview at their home the following day at 6:00 p.m. She took down the address and phone number.

Because of the experience behind the Trixos Building, Alexis had become cautious. She first verified the phone number by asking to phone back. He gave the phone number, and Alexis phoned back. In the background, she heard young male voices, which aroused her suspicion; she still agreed to go. But before she left, she asked Molly to phone Samee's house at 7:00 p.m. to make sure she was still in good shape. She gave Molly the address where she was heading for the interview. Alexis had become streetwise.

Alexis rode her bicycle to Samee's home. Another man led her in, and he said Samee and his family were on their way. He asked Alexis to wait inside. She did. Inside the house, Alexis found young men in their twenties giggling and popping their heads from another room every now and again. No other women were in the house. Something didn't seem right. The acting host offered her a drink, which she declined. He switched on the television. He disappeared to go to another room and then came back with questions to ask. Someone in that room had to be providing the questions. "What are you studying? Where are you from? How long will you be in Cyprus? Do you live on your own?" All the questions felt probing, and feisty Alexis refused to answer. She said that she would do so when Samee arrived with his family.

Then the phone rang. That had to be Samee. Was he phoning to tell her that he would be delayed? It was getting late. When would he come? Questions went around in her head. She was getting nervous. Yes, the phone was for Alexis. It was not Samee but someone who wanted to talk to her. She was handed the phone, and she gave a sigh of relief—it was Molly. Good on Molly to remember!

Alexis told her that the family was not around yet. Before Molly asked any questions, Alexis purposely mentioned the police in a sentence to frighten the boys. Some of the crowd by now had gathered in the room to listen to her conversation.

She said, "Yes, the police are aware of my visit too." This was not true, and Molly was left confused as to what Alexis was going on about.

Molly asked, "Why police? What has happened?"

"Nothing. I will explain later," replied Alexis before she gave the game away with further responses.

Alexis waited for a while. Finally, she became exasperated and got up to leave. The host quickly made a phone call and asked Samee to come home soon. She was assured again in a polite manner that the would-be employers were coming and asked to hang on, which she did. It was now 7:45 p.m., and it was getting dark. Alexis finally made a bold move and left. She did not feel safe with these young, volatile men.

When she arrived at the hostel, a fellow was on the steps smoking. She recognised him as one of the giggling team at Samee's home! He was a tenant of the noisy room above her. He had arrived at the hostel by car before her; he probably wanted to check Alexis's reaction as she came into the hostel. It then dawned on Alexis that this had been a setup either to make her into a laughingstock or to harm her! Had Molly's phone call saved her?

What dreadful men, and what an escape she had. Her alertness had saved her. The idea to verify the phone call had come from one of her business courses. So her studies had helped her be vigilant.

But who was the man in the other room requesting that those questions be asked? Was it Samee? Who was Samee then?

The following day, she phoned and asked to talk to Samee. Maybe it was him, or maybe not, as she could not differentiate the voice. She told him what she suspected and warned him that she may go to the police, just in case they tried to play this prank again. She made up her mind that this was not going to stop her from advertising, but she would not respond to young-sounding voices again. Second lesson learned!

Alexis told Molly what had happened, and she stood gaping with shocked eyes. If she had had dentures, they would have fallen out! The hitchhiking Diana Ross lost her voice for once!

Rosella

Another phone call from the same advertisement in *Destiny Weekly* brought a turnaround in Alexis's destiny! An Italian family called her up for a twice-a-week job, and she told the gentleman that she could give them Wednesdays and Fridays. He agreed to her hourly rate and occupational conditions, which she always negotiated up front on the phone to avoid haggling afterwards. She was invited for an interview.

Mr. Franco was a young, plump gentleman who had all the patience required of a man of his diplomatic position. He had a post at the Italian embassy. He talked calmly to Alexis, stopping to explain to his wife, Rosella, every now and again, as she spoke very little English—just a few words. Rosella seemed like a nervous woman. She sat with her three-year-old son, Marco, in her lap. She fidgeted with the son's toys and at the same time listened earnestly to the conversation.

He asked her, "Are you English?" A smile appeared on Mr. Franco's face. Her English accent was a giveaway.

"Well, yes, as my mother is English, but I am also Greek from my father's side," she said with assurance, feeling pumped up that a job was on the way.

Mr. Franco became interested in her personal history, and Alexis began relating information about herself. This was a diplomatic home, so they had to know all about their hopeful employee.

"Do you speak any other languages?" Mr. Franco inquired.

"Greek, which is not so polished up." Alexis quickly continued, "I am not too good at learning languages."

Alexis could sense that she had lessened his suspicion of employing a total stranger to work in a diplomat's home. His wife walked in with a coffee tray. As she served them, she talked to her husband, who turned around to speak with Alexis. "What made you come to this island for studies?"

"Well, I saw this advert in a newsletter for a business course at a British college," she continued with confidence. "And I thought it would be fascinating to go and study on a Mediterranean island and connect with my paternal roots."

He nodded his head, taking her answer well. By this time, she had a hot cup of coffee in her hand. It was Italian coffee, served in a small teacup. Alexis took her first sip. It had a fine, delightful aroma and tasted delicious. Rosella interrupted the silence, and Mr. Franco turned to Alexis to interpret what she had said. He told her that they had just moved into this house and were waiting for their furniture to come from Italy. At present, before all their possessions arrived, she was required to clean the floor and the windows. Alexis finished her coffee and began to feel at ease, but it was still not clear whether she had the job or not.

The couple took Alexis on a tour of the house. One glance at the windows and huge glass doors that opened on to the patio conveyed a direct message that she would have a tough job to make these windows see-through! They were smudged with dust because of the hot dry season, light rays bringing dust with it. The cooker, too, needed a thorough scrub, which Alexis was told was rented, together with the rest of the furniture. Besides these, the rest looked like normal spring-cleaning.

"What do you think of the work?" asked Mr. Franco.

"Oh, it seems all right," she replied with certainty.

"You said you have Wednesday and Friday free for us?" inquired Mr. Franco.

"Yes."

"Where else do you work?"

Alexis told them of the two houses she worked for on an irregular basis. Mr. Franco said he wanted to make sure that Alexis was not also working for a home from an opposing country.

Then Mr. Franco made the most desired request: "When can you start?"

Alexis was thrilled at this prospect. *Was she really getting this job?* She was excited.

"Anytime you like," she answered meekly.

It was settled that she would start work on Wednesday, 8:30 a.m. Mr. Franco turned around to ask his wife if that was okay. She was following him like a timid lamb, and their son was happily chuckling away in the kitchen.

"That's fine with us," his wife replied.

Alexis wondered how she was going to communicate with Rosella. She would need to carry a translation dictionary. At this point, she thought it was best not to ask about this just in case they changed their minds. She left hurriedly with an excuse that she had to go somewhere. Alexis realised that she would have to use a lot of hand gestures to talk to Rosella. It was going to be time-consuming.

However, she felt elated and felt like spinning on a windmill at the prospect of getting a job. She was relieved that one worry was over and now she could concentrate on her accommodation.

Molly and Bicycle

Alexis went looking for Molly the following day and told her the great news. She was elated for Alexis and teased her to take either Italian or miming lessons! It was Molly's free afternoon, and she agreed to go with Alexis to Dionys Supermarket, as she needed to fill her fridge. Molly quickly grabbed her floppy cotton sun hat; it had a bright, colourful sunflower print and created a tropical bloom on her head. Chubby Molly jumped on the back saddle; this was another form of hitchhiking, with Alexis in the riding seat in her red bucket hat. They set off laughing boisterously, Molly's legs stretched wide apart to prevent them from tangling in the spokes. The bicycle swerved every now and again. It was a sight to watch that would cheer up anyone who was feeling miserable.

It was midafternoon, and the street was quiet. Most folks were having a siesta, but it did not stop bringing one alert lady to the window. She smiled at the antics of the foreign student girls. Suddenly, Alexis and Molly heard a bang! The bicycle veered violently, and both fell to the side of the road with the bicycle on top of them. They were shocked at first, but they lifted themselves up and laughed. They had gotten away with slight bruises and grazes from the small stones. A motorbike stopped by, and the male rider shook his head at the giggling girls, and he raced off noisily.

This now meant postponing the trip to the supermarket and taking the bicycle to the repair shop. Alexis was aware that there was one in the old city of Nicosia, and this was at the other end of the city. They carried the bicycle to the main road, but the bus driver would not allow them to take the bicycle into the bus.

"Only passengers," he told them firmly.

They took a paid taxi to Elefteria Square, as nobody would have given them a lift within the city. They asked some people for directions. The two chuckling girls carried the bicycle there like a stretcher. The repair workshop was on a narrow street off Ledra Street. The tune of Greek music was keeping their minds occupied.

The repairman looked up from his work at the girls and gave a quizzical glance at Molly, as foreigners like her were rare to be seen in the area. Molly sensed it and warmed him with her patented smile, showing her white teeth. He was a bald-headed man, middle-aged, of around five and a half feet in height, and he spoke little English. He greeted them in Greek, and both answered back in Greek. Alexis showed him the ruptured tyre, speaking in Greek and English and miming, which became a combined new vernacular language for her.

"Tyre *boom*!" The repairman made a bursting sound. "How happened?" he asked in broken English.

Alexis giggled and pointed towards Molly. In her new vernacular language, she explained to him how Molly, the hitchhiking queen, thumbed a lift with her on her bicycle! He couldn't resist laughing too.

Inside the workshop, a woody scent perfumed the air. Molly asked him about it by performing a typical mime from that part of the world, to convey that the fragrance smelled good. She made smelling noises by lifting her nose, and raising her fingers in a cupped gesture, to assure him that it certainly *was* aromatic. Molly was enjoying game-playing.

He understood clearly and expressed with delight, "Aah, Hamam Turkish bath. Steam good. Oil on head good too." He stopped from his repair job and said while pointing to his bald head, "I want hair growing here."

He tried to explain what he knew in Greek, English, and fluttering hand actions. Steaming stimulated blood circulation and flushed out toxins from the skin. It helped unclog the scalp pores and encouraged hair regrowth. Combined herbal oils like those of rosemary, thyme, eucalyptus, cypress, cedar, lavender, and clary sage, if regularly massaged into the scalp and towel-wrapped in a steam room, encouraged hair growth. This was what he had been attempting outside of his bicycle repair job—fixing his thinning hair crown!

He replaced the ruptured bicycle tube with a new one, and when he had completed the job, he wagged his finger at Molly to advise her that she was not to be a passenger anymore. Molly giggled, and Alexis said loudly, "Neh," which meant *yes* in Greek, and nodded her head in agreement.

Alexis paid him the asking price, and at last she got her bicycle running again. It had been a costly repair job in total with the taxi ride and time taken over it, but from this experience, she learnt about Turkish baths and hair oils for crowning glories and no more lifts on her bicycle. Alexis rode back, and Molly returned by bus, and they arranged to meet at Dionys Supermarket. Alexis bought enough to fill her fridge with healthy food. Molly went for mouth sweeteners, which explained her bulging belly.

Chapter 4

Living in a Yoga House

While at the supermarket, Alexis saw an advertisement for a yoga exercise class, and as a result, she followed up by contacting the class, which was near the town centre, and regularly began to attend the centre. It was held in a house that was ancient and needed a good round of refurbishment. Very likely, the proprietor would one day demolish this old house, build a high-rise building, and rent out the apartments or offices.

At the Yoga Centre, Didi Maleah, the lady in charge, was a mixed Polynesian from one of the American Pacific islands, slightly older than Alexis, who also ran an English-speaking nursery school. She knew Alexis was looking for a new place and told her that her family had a spare bedroom. Didi suggested that Alexis could have it as a rent share. She added that she could also use all the available house facilities, including free yoga classes. But there were living conditions attached to it. To live there, one could not eat meat, fish, onions, or eggs in the house. Alexis needed time to think about it and could not give an immediate answer; she placed the room offer on hold.

It was the end of October, and the time arrived for Molly finally to leave the island. Alexis felt a deep pang of sadness to bid her farewell and see her depart. She said her farewell from the doorstep of the student hostel, and Molly placed her luggage in the taxi, hugged Alexis good-bye with a saddened heart, and left for the airport. Alexis now felt it was the right time for her to leave the hostel. She wanted a change to her surroundings too.

Some weeks went by, and then Alexis remembered the room offer at the Yoga Centre. She contacted Didi Maleah, who told her that the room was still available. Alexis decided to move there. She paid her first week's rent in advance and was given a quick introduction to the Yoga Centre. She was told that both men and women who gave up their entire lives for this yoga organisation lived with as few possessions as possible. After taking the vows, women were known as Didis and men as Dadas. To generate income, they ran a nursery school and yoga classes on charitable status. Alexis found out later that Didi Maleah still needed a lot of experience in running a community centre. Alexis never found out, though, what their main aim was to exist as an organisation.

Alexis packed all her belongings, together with her bicycle, into the removal van, ready to be transported to her new home, the Yoga Centre. She felt a twinge of sadness as she gave a last look at the room that had been her home for the last four years. She saw a crowd of boys' heads popping out from the upstairs balcony window as they watched her leave. As the van drove round the bend, she gave a final look at the building and saw the same fellow from Samee's prank advertisement watching from the balcony window; maybe he was feeling guilty for making Alexis leave that place.

The Yoga Centre may have looked inviting from the outside, but once Alexis got inside, it was to turn pickle for her. Alexis had been naive about her new housemate!

On arrival at the Yoga Centre in the afternoon, Didi Maleah met Alexis. All her previous sweetness melted away, and Alexis was confronted by an icy, unknown character whose personality blended with the wintry January weather. What a phony pony she had turned out to be!

Without even welcoming Alexis, Didi exclaimed, "I can smell fish here. I told you that you will not be eating any fish here!"

She was right. Alexis had a fish tin that got packed away by mistake, even though she had made a special attempt to be free from all of the disallowed items. She was aghast at Didi's approach, but Alexis was not going to remain quiet.

"Is this the way to welcome a person? Couldn't you have asked me in a better tone?" Alexis lashed out to let Didi know that she was not going to allow herself to be trampled over. It quickly dawned on Didi that there was little chance of making Alexis her subject.

Alexis felt deceived and let down. She couldn't go back to her hostel room, as it was already booked by another student. What a mistake she had made, and now she would have to get through it. She felt angry at being lured into the situation.

Didi continued with her hollering. "You are not to use the electric heater, and if you like, you can take this table to your room." She showed Alexis the table in the sitting room that was used for their meetings. She continued with her lamenting. "And place your bicycle in the back porch."

"What's wrong with the front porch?" Alexis asked her in a firm tone.

"It doesn't look nice," came the fiery reply.

Alexis knew that she was trying to show her who was going to be the boss here, but Alexis had to remind Didi that she was the joint tenant, as she was paying half the rent.

Alexis blurted out, "Instead of blabbering away with your rules, why don't you first help me take my luggage to my room?"

The luggage consisted of a couple of small boxes and two suitcases. The weather was hot, which would make anyone short-tempered in a situation like this. Didi came to Alexis's help reluctantly, thumping the boxes onto the floor.

When the rent agreement was made verbally, Didi had promised to give Alexis a bed, mattress, and cupboard, which were nowhere to be seen. The bed was all detached and lying in the storeroom at the back of the house. Both girls brought it out from there and set it up for the night, using spare, clean bedsheets and blankets. At least Alexis had a roof over her head for the night, but she went to sleep with a heavy heart.

Alexis woke up at four in the morning with rain pouring heavily on the rooftop, which sounded more like rocks falling on it than rain. At her previous place, she had never heard the rain fall, as there was a flat above her. All of a sudden, she remembered her bicycle, which was her precious property together with her college books. She rushed out of her room and out through the front door onto the porch, only to find her bicycle all drenched in the rain. Didi had removed it from the front porch and placed it out in the open in the front garden!

Alexis had forgotten to take it to the back porch, as they had to set up the bed, a task that Didi should have dealt with in the first place before she arrived.

Alexis ran out in the rain and pulled her bicycle onto the porch. She did not even have her shoes on. She was desperate to save her bicycle. This was the first time she had seen her bicycle have a "taste" of rain. It was always left under the protection of a roof. Alexis concluded that there was a limit to tolerance! Alexis went berserk and, without thinking straight, barged into Didi's room. She was fast asleep in a sleeping bag on the floor with the kerosene heater still on; she had forgotten to switch it off. She was an absent-minded person.

Did Didi care about Alexis's belongings? No, she did not. How could she place value on other people's possessions when she had none of her own to care about? Alexis went into a rage. She pulled Didi out of her sleeping bag and shook her, shouting and screaming. She picked up Didi's clothing, shoes, pillow, and whatever came into her hand, and she threw them out from the window into the rain.

"You couldn't let me place my bicycle in the front porch—then what kind of charity work do you do?" Alexis yelled at her. "What harm would it have done to you to allow it to remain on the front porch for the night? Plus, you could have asked me to put it on the back porch! You are false!"

Alexis went wild. She did not even know what she was doing. Didi did not say a word. She remained silent and avoided Alexis by running into the sitting room. She was frightened.

Alexis continued to holler. "Before removing any of my property, ask me first!"

Alexis had become uncontrollable, and Didi fled for her life, picking up her saved night slippers on the way out into the rain. She went to spend the night at their nursery school. Alexis had a good mind to go after her there too! She didn't. Dawn had broken, and Alexis had to go to work.

The yoga leader was like a live turkey on the run from hungry hands!

Days rolled by. Alexis's life revolved around studies at the library, work, and daily squabbles back at home. She and Didi never became friends. Didi did not want to evict her, as she needed the money and it was difficult to find a housemate, as one would not want to live in an old house. Alexis was in search of new accommodations.

Alexis just lived her own life in that house, paid rent, and did not care or have the time to bother about Didi's presence. She did not even join in the yoga activities held in the sitting room. She watched and heard the familiar pretentious, sweet tone coming from Didi Maleah as she mingled with her students. They all thought the world of her and took to her like a duck to water. Alexis never even tried telling anyone attending the Yoga Centre what had happened. They must have already heard Didi's version of it, and nothing was going to change it—not even a thunderous voice from heaven!

For rent, Alexis would leave an envelope on the kitchen tabletop and stand there to see Didi open the packet and count it. For the bathroom and kitchen, Alexis waited for her to finish using these rooms before heading in that direction. Didi clearly wanted to be Alexis's boss, but this was not going to be possible with the feisty bicycle lady. Didi's hope had been that Alexis would become submissive to her and become part of the yoga movement, clanging two cymbals against each other while going in a dance circle and repeating the lyrical words. This did not appeal to Alexis at all; in the past, she had only been interested in the physical exercise part of it. Alexis was strong minded and knew what she wanted. Instead, Didi got a "clang-clang" of cymbals behind her ears to wake her up to the etiquette of sharing life and not controlling it!

Olynasa Pub and the Invite

The tiffs at the Yoga Centre drove Alexis to a well-known pub, Olynasa, which also had a café. This became one of the places where foreigners gathered, especially the United Nations soldiers. It was an opportunity to meet people and exchange ideas and views. In fact, Alexis started to gain knowledge about different countries. She occasionally took wine, enough to enjoy it but not get drunk. These men would try to get her to take more so she would get drunk, but she was resistant to following the tide; she knew her boundaries. Alexis remembered Molly and how silly she behaved under the influence of alcohol; it had made everyone laugh at her. Molly created a spectacle of herself. Alexis did not want to be in that same situation. She missed Molly and could not find another fun-lover like her. This was a small place, and it was hard to find someone like her.

Christmas was nearing, and Mrs. Williams invited Alexis to her home for tea. Alexis knew she was up to something as soon as she arrived, for Mrs. Williams had a funny sparkle in her eye. She entertained while her husband, Paul, kept busy taking care of their three children. He did not engage much with the guests. Alexis realized Mrs. Williams wanted her to meet their friend Stefan over a Christmas get-together. He was a young man from Holland, a country of windmills. He was a big, well-built man, with thick-framed glasses, and he had a beard. He worked for an offshore firm; he looked more like a fisherman! But Alexis was not interested. She had her eyes set on someone else, but had placed him on hold due to her studies.

Alexis glared at him purposely so that he would dislike her and not pursue her. She did not want to offend her employer and hoped this would end amiably. They had been good to her in giving her a job, and to be polite, she stuck around until it was time to go. Mrs. Williams got the hint, and so did the "fisherman" invitee, to her delight.

Alexis had a mixed reaction to the invitation, as she was disappointed that Mrs. Williams had not consulted her first. She comically thought that Mrs. Williams should open up a matchmaking agency and give it a catchy name—Divine Fishing Rod. Her slogan could be "Divine Fishing Rod hooks you up!"

Alexis was still living in the yoga house. The winter days were cold and windy with draughts coming in through the edges of the window. Alexis would wake up early in the morning shivering, and the first thing she had to do was switch on the kerosene heater. Cycling to work was enjoyable, as it left her feeling mentally refreshed and warm.

Work with the Italian family was going fine. Rosella always seemed happy to see her and greeted, "*Como stai*," or "Good morning," and Alexis gave her a reply accordingly. If their son, Marco, was still around, then it meant the little imp had managed to escape going to the nursery school. He was a mischievous little boy, full of laughter, and could pretend to be ill if he wished not to go to a place, which included the nursery school.

He disliked going to the one he was registered with, which was a private English-speaking one. Parents who could afford it would choose an English-speaking nursery so their children would learn English from a young age. The nursery, oddly enough, was the one the Yoga Centre managed. Alexis found this out when Rosella mentioned the name Didi and the nursery school, and Alexis put these two together. Alexis did not divulge to Rosella her connection to the nursery school owners to avoid being asked sensitive questions, and Alexis did not know either if Didi was aware of her work with the Francos. This left Alexis feeling uncomfortable at times.

After a short time Marco was transferred to another nursery, where he seemed happy and willing to go. But Alexis was still stuck at the Yoga Centre; she could not find another accommodation. Fate had to take its own twist, and it did. Alexis one day wrote her thoughts on a piece of paper as a way to vent her feelings about her dislike of the place and mentioned that Didi was a fake. Alexis meant to tear up that piece of paper and throw it away, but she forgot it, and it flew from her window onto the outside garden grounds. And who had to see it? It wasn't the postman or the yoga devotees, but Didi herself! It was destined to be seen by her.

In the evening, Didi confronted Alexis, and Alexis stood there in an unfearful manner and did not deny it. Alexis wanted to show her that she was not going to be submissive to her, as she was making her followers do; vulnerable people fell for the trap, and Alexis did not hide to mention this. That day, Didi asked Alexis to leave and she was given one month to do so.

Professor Edgar

She desperately needed a new home now. Help came her way when Mrs. Williams referred her to an American professor of sociology. He was Professor Edgar. Mrs. Williams was pleased with Alexis's timely work and spoke well of her to Professor Edgar, who offered her a job. Mrs. Williams still kept in touch with Alexis for irregular work for Tuesdays, as this day suited her most, and so did Mr. Sophoclis for any free day. But Alexis had one thing most on her mind at present, and that was to move out from the Yoga Centre.

Professor Edgar was in his late fifties. He was an active, single man and had no wrinkles on his face. Alexis worked for him on alternate Saturdays. His handwriting had become squiggly, so he had to type out most of his written work, including the weekly work schedule for Alexis. He was a quiet person and did not bother Alexis with her work. Usually, he would go off and leave her alone in the flat. But when he was around, she enjoyed talking to him. Very soon, she asked him if he knew of any vacant place, as she needed to move out from the Yoga Centre.

Since Professor Edgar worked in a college, he was able to obtain information for her for rented accommodation. There was one available near the Green Line in a two-storey block of student bedsit flats with its own balcony as well as a communal rooftop veranda. The flat was lined with the common marble flooring, and the staircase was marbled to provide coolness when the weather was hot. She phoned the proprietor, Mr. Nikolas Pachis, and met him. His surname meant *fat* in Greek, and he, in fact, was a stocky man, clean-shaven with wavy, shoulder-length hair combed backwards.

He showed her the flat and asked her questions to get an idea of how long she would stay.

"Indefinitely," she replied.

The flat was a larger bedsit with its own kitchen, landline telephone, and balcony, which suited Alexis, and she inquired about the noise from his tenants.

To this, he said in an assured tone, "No, I only rent to civilised people and hope you will be one too." Alexis was extremely relieved.

The rent was reasonable, and he insisted on a deposit with the first rent to secure the flat. Alexis accepted it, but she had to come back the following day with the whole amount, as she did not have it on her. When she did, she got the keys, along with a lecture on the importance of looking after the property, paying monthly rent at the end of the month, not creating noise, and contacting him for the repairs. She did not need to ask him for his phone number, as she already had it.

Alexis was ready to move. She informed Didi by writing a note and left it in the kitchen with a saltshaker used as a weight over the note, so it would not fly off. Rent was paid already, so she was free to leave. Alexis felt greatly elated. She was excited about moving to her new place. Finally, the day came for her to leave the Yoga Centre, but Didi was nowhere to be seen. Didi had performed a disappearing act! She sent a gentleman from her yoga group to collect the keys.

Sarcastically, Alexis queried, "What happened to Didi? Did she get lost in a trance?"

The gentleman did not respond. He was aware of their domestic war and remained tight-lipped. Didi was like a saint to her followers.

What a sigh of relief, she handed the keys over. She had a last look in the room to see if she had left anything, as she did not want to come back for it. Then she got into the removal van and headed for the Green Line flat. Alexis settled down quickly in her new, modern place. By now she was as familiar with moving as Molly was with hitchhiking.

Chapter 5

Alexis's New Home

A lexis's bedsit was situated on the edge of the Green Line. From the rooftop balcony, she could see in the distance the rundown row of street buildings on the northern side of Cyprus and figures of Turkish soldiers manning their side of the occupied land. One of the United Nations barracks was situated in no-man's-land, and it was to be Alexis's new neighbour. She could see these United Nations soldiers sunbathing and some stripping naked to get an even tan. A few young, cheeky ones would make gestures towards their naked private parts while she was gazing from the balcony. Pictures were not allowed in this sensitive area, or she would have taken some. What a photo album it would have been!

Alexis got along with her new landlord, Mr. Pachis, and addressed him by his first name, Nikolas. He had a good sense of humour. He was a British university graduate, and it seemed they were on the same wavelength to some extent. He once came to repair the rooftop balcony wall, and she heard the commotion. Alexis suspected it must be him, and she went out onto the balcony to talk to him. He had a brush in his hand and was smiling while sweeping off dust and cobwebs from a huge, chest-length gas cylinder.

Alexis joked, "That's a big girl you've got there."

He looked at it with a question in his eyes, smiled, and nodded.

"Are you combing her long hair?" continued Alexis, being comical.

He just laughed. "This is for an emergency to make the generator work if the electricity gets cut off." He pointed to the generator nearby.

He asked her how she was settling down while brushing his well-rounded "gas girl." Alexis conveyed to him that she was adjusting and appreciated being in her new place.

A respectable business relationship was building between these two. Alexis did not want distraction from her exams or to face eviction if the landlord-tenant relationship went sour. She was being cautious. Her mind was set for a younger Swedish officer from the United Nations. His name was Sven Karlsson, and she had met him at Olynasa Pub a few times and had a quick chat with him.

All was going well for Alexis now. House tensions were gone. According to her, every part of her life was falling into place. She was filled with glee. As she cycled past the nearby jolly shopkeepers from the street, she would cheerfully shout out a greeting at them or visit them for a laugh when their wives were not around. She knew if a woman was around by looking through the glass window. If one was around, then that woman could only be his protective wife. She felt that she could now see happy days ahead.

Alexis's daily work was normal domestic work like any other housewife's duty. The only thing she did not consider was cooking. She enjoyed admiring her work and creating a clean, shining touch. After polishing a piece of furniture or brassware, she would look from a distance to see how it shone and put in more effort if it didn't. She would go out of the room and observe whether the small carpets were aligned properly.

At the Franco house, she would even forget about her coffee break until Rosella called her. There was always something satisfying to eat, which gave her the energy to carry on with her work until lunchtime, when they would have a friendly "chat," with hand-waving gestures, miming, and constant use of the Italian-English dictionary. Rosella's drama class was in progress!

Whenever the phone rang, Rosella would rush for it as if there were a burglar in her house and, in desperation, she reached to the phone for help! The phone calls were numerous, and most of them were callers with whom

Rosella would get angry. Her husband phoned her every now and again, probably to convince her that he was definitely coming home that evening!

One day, Alexis heard her saying in broken English, "You want what?" There was a pause, and then she squealed, "Whisky?" She slammed the phone down.

Alexis rushed to the bathroom to laugh her head off. Rosella came looking for her, just in time to find Alexis pretending to clean the mirror. She told her in broken English about her telephone conversation with a lady who said that she wanted whisky. Alexis understood here and there, and to keep Rosella happy, she nodded her head in agreement. Rosella headed straight for the phone to warn her husband about the telephone conversation she just had regarding "whisky." There was certainly a misunderstanding with the Greek language, and the husband must have reassured her that no woman would take her place!

Working for Rosella was fun, though Alexis had to learn to be patient with her. At last, their furniture arrived in a freight lorry. The furniture was all beautiful Italian-manufactured pieces, including two huge pianos, one for the son and one for the father, skiing gear, and...well, name a modern equipment of its time, and they had it. With the arrival of the cargo, there was no shortage of work. The house was small for their possessions. They must have lived in a double-storey mansion before. It had to be crammed up; there were bookshelves in the corridor too.

Alexis had been working for Rosella for some months now, and it was around Easter. The job was sadly to be short-lived.

Alexis went to Olynasa Pub, and here she would chat with the pub's chef, but mostly she hoped that the Swedish officer was in town. Michael, the chef, and the bartender would come out for a break to the veranda area and enjoy a cigarette when it was not too busy. To survive the heat from the massive stove, they let out the steam through their mouths in the form of dirty jokes, which, after some time, Alexis became used to and became a laughing audience for these sit-down comedians.

Michael was in his midthirties; he was of mixed race, Puerto Rican and Greek. The islanders were getting used to Greek men living abroad and sending mixed-race children back to Cyprus or bringing them back to settle down on the island. Alexis was one of them too, so she could relate to him. They held more Westernised views, though, than did the local ones. Michael introduced Latin American music to the playlist, which was regularly played, and people would get up and dance wherever they found floor space to do so.

Alexis would go and talk to Michael about her problems. He was a comfort when she lived in the Yoga Centre. But this time, she came under the wrong influence of this young chef over wages. He felt what Alexis was getting from the Francos was little, and he told her to ask for a wage increase. It was her first regular work, and the amount she had quoted to Mr. Franco was less than the amount she charged Professor Edgar. She had not given a sensible thought to it and had gotten carried away in order to get the job.

Alexis felt embarrassed to ask Rosella in person for a rate increase, so she wrote a note and placed it under the door. She felt she could express much better in writing than conversing. If she had asked, she would have stammered and not come across well. After leaving the note, she began to dread the outcome.

Wednesday morning came. She was stopped at the door by a note! It was stuck on the door and read that Rosella did not need her anymore. Alexis stood there motionless. She certainly did not expect this. She was numb and could not think straight. She took the note from the door. She felt she had been unfairly treated for asking. She wrote a note and got back a note. This was a tit-for-tat match. The chef had advised her, but he should have guided her into how to go about it too! She got misled, and what a lesson she learned. She couldn't even ride the bicycle. Alexis had to walk with it, heading towards her flat. She felt she still had to talk to Mr. Franco about this. What she had done began to sink in, and she felt a great regret welling up inside her.

The following day, Alexis phoned Mr. Franco at his office, since his wife could not communicate in English, and asked him where she had gone wrong. He informed her that it was because she had written a note that offended his wife. It would have been better if she had asked verbally. To this, Alexis gave a sigh of relief. Alexis explained her side of the story and the reason she had written a note rather than request verbally. She also said she felt embarrassed for having done so, as Rosella had been good to her. He listened patiently. He was very understanding and told her that he would try to do something about it. But, oh no, Rosella did not want to see her! Rosella was hurt. This had not been Alexis's intention. Alexis could not understand why Rosella would not accept an apology. She refused adamantly with no chance of return.

Alexis decided to accept her destiny, as the name of the newspaper was where she was placing her advertisements regularly. She walked about with a bottled-up feeling of regret for a long time, but learned something new: the etiquette of dealing with employers. She had to talk to them in person. Also, she could not be led by others so easily, even if they were in a higher position or older than she was. The chef surely overcooked her plate!

The exams were in six weeks' time, and she decided not to add any more jobs to her schedule. She placed the advertisement in the newspaper on hold. She would use her free time to study, as she had to pass her exams this time around. Mrs. Williams still called her on an irregular basis, and in a comforting tone, she advised her to concentrate on her studies now.

"I have been studying," assured Alexis. "Very hard, too."

Mrs. Williams wanted her to pass her exams and felt Alexis needed mature guidance.

Mr. Sophoclis, the suspicious journalist, had stopped calling her for work; probably he had become a stowaway in a spaceship. Up in space he would have nobody to be distrustful of! Professor Edgar was still busy typing out her work list. At least Alexis was not destitute; she had savings, a crutch for her to lean on. Now was the time to get her nose stuck in her books and get disciplined with it.

Chapter 6

New Landlord and New Jobs

Alexis's landlord had a habit of delaying repairs. The rejection note on the Franco family's door was an educational wake-up call, and she decided to use this same tactic on her new landlord. Alexis felt he needed a strong dose to alert him mentally, as she had received from the Francos.

Alexis ended up having a plumbing problem at her flat that disrupted her studies; her shower had a drain blockage. She tried a gutter plunger and used liquid chemical, both to no avail. Alexis rang her landlord, and he lazily agreed to come round. But he didn't. During this time, Alexis managed to have a manual shower by using a plastic container and scooping water onto her body. It was getting laborious, plus taking up her precious study time. She phoned the landlord a couple of times, but he gave the same promise that he would pop round to repair it, but he didn't. It was soon to be the end of the month, and the landlord was to make his visit to gather the rent. She waited for this chance to let him know what she was made of. She stuck a note on the door! It read, "No repairs. No rent. You keep to your side of the agreement, and I will keep to mine. Alexis."

Mr. Pachis came striding in, carrying his stocky body up the stairs to collect his rent, and read the note. He knocked on the door—maybe he took it as a joke, but Alexis was not fooling about. She opened the door and pointed to the note. He asked to come inside to see the problem. Still in silence, she showed him the shower that was filled with water. The landlord was amused at all this. She broke her silence.

"You should have done this ages ago. Get the tools or plumber, or no rent," she informed him firmly.

"So you can still talk?" the landlord remarked jovially.

"I talk when I need to," came the sarcastic reply.

The landlord left empty-handed, the landlord left empty-handed, and Alexis did not know if he would return.

He surely did and came back with the tools. The threat worked. He was not a plumber, and Alexis wondered if he could even unscrew the plughole! He tried the plunger, which Alexis had already used, and it still did not work. He got on his hands and knees to work. At last he was labouring. He unscrewed the plughole and placed a plumber's snake into the drain hole to hook the clog. He pulled out a stash of black hair and blamed Alexis for it.

She quickly retorted, "Remember that I do not have black hair. I am legally brunette, and I always wear a shower cap." She continued in a questioning, playful tone, "Perhaps the previous tenant had black hair, hey?"

Mr. Pachis, still in a kneeling position, did not want to expand on this, so he joined in with laughter. Alexis, out of mischief, took a plunger and placed it close to his right ear and mimicked a plunging action, and did the same with the left ear.

"Clean your ears and *listen.*" She emphasised the last word. Alexis was having fun with her new landlord, and he was having fun with her. He, too, was playing a teasing game with her. She then thought of a spiteful game to play.

"I have this tea that cleanses the body. Do you want to try it?" She held out a packet to him.

"Will it cleanse my ears?" the landlord asked teasingly while still working on the shower and giving it a finishing touch.

"Why don't you try and see for yourself," Alexis said from the kitchen, while boiling water for the tea.

Mr. Pachis just wanted to hang around for more fun, and the stocky mouse fell for the bait! She chuckled under her breath at the thought of what was to come.

He got Alexis's shower working again, stood up, and washed his hands. Alexis gave him his rent, and he sat down for his tea. Alexis joined in too, as she also wanted an herbal cleansing. As soon as he finished his tea, she got him out of her flat quick with an excuse of studies. She did not want him to get stuck using the bathroom in her flat, as she knew he would need it soon. It was laxative tea!

She saw him after some days in a shop, downstairs, and he commented with a circular hand gesture on his stomach, "That tea of yours was a real washout. I was stuck at home for a day to complete that cleansing of yours." She could only giggle at this.

As she cycled off chuckling with delight, she called out to him, "Remember, I got stuck too without a working shower." She didn't tell him that it was a laxative cleanser mixed in tea!

Alexis focused on her studies. She needed a fan to keep cool, as the days were warm. As the exam date got nearer, she concentrated fully on her studies. To relax her brain, she would pop into Olynasa Pub to have a chat with Michael. Exam date came, and Alexis had a healthy breakfast but no eggs, and she entered the exam hall, nervous and anxious. All faces around her were tense. The future depended on this; some had to meet their parents' expectations. Alexis searched for the seat with her name on it. She found it near a row of large windows, which thankfully had shutters to keep the sunrays out. She looked around her; some looked dishevelled with stress-lined faces, and some were dressed to impress, not a hint of exam nerves. Several were chewing gum due to nerves (which research suggested improved test performance), while others drank bottled water they had carried due to the heat. Nobody was allowed to talk. The adrenaline was pumping fast to get the body ready for action. Alexis was advised by her college tutor to write her emotions down before the exams, as it helped to calm the nerves, and she followed the suggestion. The two exam invigilators, a middle-aged man and woman, were watching from the front with eagle eyes.

Then one got up and announced loudly, so that she could be heard at the back of the hall, "All paper and books should be out of sight now.

Put them below your chair. Nothing should be on your desk except for the writing instruments." There was a crinkling noise of paper, books shutting with a low thud, and chairs being dragged closer to the desks as students adjusted in their seats.

The invigilators cut open the large brown envelope containing the exam papers, removed the pile from it, and began handing them out to each one, facing downwards. All one could hear now was the rustle of papers and the invigilators' footsteps. Some students began to breathe heavily.

"Read the exam papers properly and good luck," the male invigilator bid them in his roaring voice.

Students flipped their exam paper to the front and began. The exam invigilators paced the floor in their quiet rubber soles to check that the candidates were not cheating. Alexis toyed with her ballpoint pen to think of the answers, trying to recall the information from the memory lobe in her brain. When she did, she dug her nose hurriedly back into her paperwork, writing or calculating under the pressure of the ticking clock.

After an hour and half, the proclamation boomed at the back and front of the hall: "Time's up. Put your pens down now." Everyone did, under the watchful eyes of the invigilators. The supervisors quickly walked down the row to collect the papers.

This was to be the norm for the two-and-a-half-week period. Alexis sat for the four subjects she had to pass. The final day came, and Alexis at last handed in her last exam sheet. It was with a jubilant good-bye to college books and a welcoming hello to sunshine, sea, and dating.

Hooray, the ordeal was over. Alexis was free from studying, and it was summer again. She now felt ready to meet her admirer, the Swedish officer. Michael, the chef, had informed her of his sightings at the pub; he also secretly updated Sven about Alexis. He was that "fishing rod hooking up," but this time welcomed by Alexis. Alexis was aware that it would be a while before the officers would be back. The Swedish officers were based in Famagusta, in northern Cyprus, which was a distance away for these lads to come to Nicosia.

Alexis had to find more work now. She was not free from its worries. Office work was difficult to find, and she decided it was best to wait for her results first. She was back at the newspaper office to advertise. She had become a regular sight there. The same man, Leon, was behind the desk, and he still looked as though he questioned whether Alexis had the ability to do the job because of the constant advertisements. But at least it brought income to their business and an increase in the bubblegum sales!

The advertisement brought no callers, and she checked whether the phone number in the advertisement was accurate. It was. After two weeks, she placed the advertisement again. Anxiously, she waited. It was cheerful news this time round, as it brought in a few callers. They were all women, and this meant these jobs were going to be serious with housewives; unlike men who at times wanted to mess around. All of the women—Wilfreda, Mrs. Ekstrom, and Susan—wanted a regular schedule. Wilfreda got Wednesdays, Mrs. Ekstrom reserved for a half-day on Thursdays, which was delayed for some weeks, and Susan accepted Fridays.

Her lifeline, Mrs. Williams, increased the frequency for housekeeping, as she began to have a steady flow of guests from abroad. She asked for Tuesdays to become a regular day for the summer period. Alexis now was fully occupied with free time on Mondays, Thursday mornings, alternate Saturdays, and Sundays.

Wilfreda

Wilfreda was a chubby German lady who had short dark-brown hair down to her neckline. She had initially wanted a Saturday job but that was gone now, so she settled for Wednesdays. She asked for references, which Professor Edgar was pleased to give, and Alexis was hired.

The German brunette was a schoolteacher and she was antichemicals. She taught German and French. The cleaning day was on her day off from school, and she opened the door to Alexis in her nightwear and uncombed hair. On the first day, Alexis met her husband and never saw him again. He was present only to give his approval or not, and

Alexis seemed to have won it. He was a quiet man with a thinning crown. Perhaps Wilfreda did not allow him to use hair oil, as it had chemicals in it! They did not have children, and if she did have, very likely it would be a home birth and the invisible atoms in the room would be petrified to even interact with each other!

Wilfreda was on a mental warpath with the chemical industries. She felt that human beings were killing the plants and trees by using too much of the chemicals. She would only allow very few drops of domestic detergents, including in the toilet. Wilfreda stood by as Alexis poured the liquid chemical into the toilet bowl. And, sure enough, her toilet bowl was tarnished brown, and Alexis needed her muscles to remove the stains.

"Just a few drops," Wilfreda would say.

Very little chemical went into the bowl, which left a dank odour. The wooden and vinyl floor was mopped with only water, as, according to "green" Wilfreda, the chemicals went into the earth later! Yes, it was a chemical-free home, and a welcome mat should have read, "Welcome to a chemical-free home, but sorry, I am musty."

At the back of the house, Wilfreda had her "eco comrades," a good-sized, unkempt garden consisting of orange trees and rectangular earthenware pots of green garnishes. Maybe in Alexis's absence she talked to them, complaining of the human race! The green vegetation must have welcomed her with open arms to their chlorophyll club and bowed down to her with great respect whenever she passed by, especially the weeds; this is the reason why they were still in her garden. She had a mission on this earth, and that was to fight for the rights of the green vegetation!

Susan

Susan's Friday home was a noisy, animal-dominated environment; it was more like a farmhouse on the outskirts of town. It had two enclosed verandas, one in the front and one at the back. Susan was a singer and woke up just before lunch, as she worked in the evenings. When she came downstairs, she would come and have a peep at Alexis and say hi to her in a perky voice, and then she greeted her animals in her chirpy singing voice. Her extended family consisted of a cat, a dog, a parrot, rabbits, a coop full of chickens, a husband, and two children from her previous marriage.

The cat roamed freely, and the long-haired pooch followed Susan at her heels. The parrot was in a cage and was allowed to fly in the house, under supervision. The rabbits were outside lazing or running up and down in a wooden, two-storey green hutch. In the large backyard, Susan's family also had an open-air enclosed chicken run. The fenced protection kept the stray dogs and feral cats out.

The chicken coop contained two wooden chicken houses, one for the hen and the chicks and one for the rooster. The hen's house was painted in yellow with a circle in golden-red on the door, and the rooster's had a door painted in reverse: golden-red with a yellow circle on it. This setup was to send an inviting message to the opposite poultry sex! The rooster's home also had a ladder to enable him to reach the rooftop to perch there to protect the territory. A homely environment was created for the animals.

Back in the house, the husband kept to himself in the front veranda. The children joined Susan in the afternoon in the back veranda for homework. They kept on giggling, as there would be an abrupt interlude of her talking to the animals. When they finished their homework, they went to join their stepfather. Alexis did ironing in the corner of the large veranda and could not help joining in with their chuckles. She wondered if they were better off with a paid tutor in the front veranda with the door closed from the wandering animals and bird, and, of course, from their mother too.

Susan's husband commented once when Alexis was having her tea break, "This is a zoo." He seemed tense as he strolled into the kitchen to have a bite. Alexis laughed to relax the uptight atmosphere.

The home was not free from animal droppings, and Susan would hurriedly clean up the mess with an angry squeal. "Eeeeeeeeh." The animals ran, probably whimpering to themselves. What could she expect when she hadn't done any poo training?

Susan was a blond lady in her midforties, with a dark, protruding mole on her upper lip, on the right side. She was highly strung, and to top this, she pinned her hair upwards at the back, which fanned out like a palm tree.

She did not stop acting and singing. She sang to her animals and danced with them. She gave names to her animals—Candy for her female African grey parrot, Chico for her male long-haired Chihuahua, Calysmeow for her female Aphrodite cat, and for her Dutch rabbits, she gave Dutch names: Kool (Dutch for *cabbage*) for the male and Kropsia (Dutch for *lettuce*) for the female! Her hen was named Penny, as it laid "pennies" for them, referring to the eggs. The rooster was known as Romulus. Romulus was building a "Rome" with his hen, Penny—a chicken city!

Susan would sing their names to them and create a song out of their combined names: "Candy, Chico, Calys-m-e-o-w. Kool, Kropsia, Romulus, and P-e-n-n-y." Her parrot, Candy, squawked "Sooosaan," and Susan would repeat her name back and occasionally get up to do a ballroom dance with the parrot sitting perched on her arm. She had begun to train her dog to dance to instrumental music. Singing Susan made the dog jump over her arm, go around her heels, and go in between her legs. It was noisy wherever she went, in or outside the house, with the combined singing and laughter alongside the dog yapping, parrot screeching, cat purring, hen clucking, and cock crowing. It was a singing animal home. Alexis found Susan's singing voice beautiful.

The singer fed her feathered and furred companions well, bathed her fur friends with a kindly touch in an animal's tub, made dinner for her family, and left the cleaning to Alexis. Alexis made her own sandwiches from items laid out on the kitchen table, and she made sure that she ate her snack from a clean, wiped table. She enjoyed working there.

When there was a birthday in the house, Susan would dress her non-talking companions too: fascinators for her female animals or bow ties for the male ones. The bright, mauve, feathery fascinators were held on a waistband, and on the collar bands sat the satin bow ties, which had a sideways zebra print on them. Even the male dog and female cat played together playfully in this house. They were both cute and a delightful sight to watch when they teased each other.

The children spent most of their time, besides homework time, with their stepfather in the front room, away from Susan and her animals. Alexis did have her own space too, as the rooms she approached had to be emptied first of animals and human beings so she could dust, wipe the furniture, mop the floors, and have a tranquil time to herself. By the end of the afternoon, the animals became tired, and they retired to their sleeping corners, but not nutty fruitcake Susan. She didn't get tired. Her recipe for energy was to keep on singing!

As soon as Alexis's work was over, which was late afternoon, she changed from her working clothes, got on her bicycle, and headed home to wait for the phone call from Sven. She had a shower, ate a proper meal, and made a quick cycle ride to Olynasa Pub to have a chat with Michael, if he was available to do so. She never needed to worry about locking her bike or balcony door, as it was really safe. Michael now had a regular female visitor in the pub. Her name was Marsha.

Chapter 7

Andreas and Olynasa Pub

Mrs. Williams's household was a busy one, and due to lack of time, she began to order her groceries by phone or in person, which were later delivered. Dionys Supermarket had a greengrocers section too, and they employed Andreas Sarafian to deliver the goods in his tricycle cart. When he was not making grocery rounds, he activated a small gas fridge to sell ice cream to the public.

Andreas was in the same age group as Alexis, a plumpish and bubbly fellow with black curly hair and an innocent-looking face, which made old ladies want to pinch his cheeks. He was a likeable person; children loved him. He was of an Armenian background. There was a large group of Armenians living on the Greek speaking side of Cyprus, following the Turkish invasion.

Andreas had a colourful tricycle cart. Over his tricycle seat, he had a blue canopy with a yellow scalloped hanging fringe to keep the heat out. Behind his tricycle, he pulled a blue cart that had a blue canopy similar to the yellow scalloped hanging fringe; the cart was a decorative sight. He even placed bunting around the cart box. If one placed a white chair in it, the cart box was large enough to transport a village bride to the church or a mayor to the town hall! On the side of the roof hung a banner that read, "Dionys Supermarket—We sell organic vegetables and fruit too." This certainly would have gained one more nonchemical customer— Wilfreda, of course! But, unfortunately, she was not living in the area.

On the right-hand side of the tricycle, there was a bugle that Andreas would sound mischievously when he passed young girls. Some felt embarrassed, and some ignored, giggled, or waved at him. He stopped by to talk or sell ice cream to some. He became known in the area as "the bugle man." He was a joyful young man on his wheels, which he said was his gym. But one day, he sounded his bugle at a wrong passer-by; she was a fuming old lady on the side pavement. She was in no mood to tug his fleshy cheeks! Andreas had one glance at her, and he rode off fast, flexing his muscles to get away from her.

The angry elderly lady was dragging an empty shopping trolley, and she ran after Andreas, shouting and lifting the trolley like a javelin. He turned around to see her running after him, and off he sped from the angry bear. He talked to his legs, asking them to spin fast, and to his body to keep it in balance. On that day, he was wearing a Superman costume, well fitting for this event. He did not want to get the wrath of that "javelin" or invite it into his cart. Fortunately, he did not have a heavy load to pull on that day, and he managed to get away from her, sweating.

He kept on cycling on this long stretch of road until her shouting voice faded away in the distance. When he felt safe to look around, he stopped to look behind him. There she was, still on the road, with her hand on one hip and the other on the handle of her trolley. She watched him from a distance with glaring eyes. A car drove up the road, stopped in front of her, and hooted for her to move. She picked up her empty trolley again, shoving the "javelin" in the air towards the car. After some time she moved, grumbling all the while, out of the way onto the side pavement. The driver of the car and the passengers all enjoyed amusement while driving off, and a hyena laughter from one of the passengers sounded in the air.

This irate old lady was Grandma Cordelia. She was of medium height with strong bones. A gutsy elderly lady, she wore a high, voluminous hair bun, which looked like a bird's nest! While he was looking back, and although a safe distance away, Andreas dared wave good-bye to her and provoked her again, as he knew he was bound to meet her again one day in this unpopulated area. Andreas's bugle had certainly triggered an angry streak in this angry steak! Surprisingly, her hair bun was still in place, well secured with hairpins, probably firmly and fiercely placed in such a manner that must have kept it from toppling over.

When he made his delivery rounds or worked as an ice cream peddler, Andreas would dress in different novelty costumes, from jolly clown, mischievous elf, flying Superman, and sea robber pirate to cuddly animals—as long as he could cycle in it. Alexis was told that around one Christmas, he came dressed in red-and-green elf top and trousers, with an elf hat that was half-red and half-green. He played a flute, and children danced around him. It was a pre-Christmas treat.

Andreas's employer had made an arrangement for him to rent novelty costumes from a fancy dress shop in Nicosia. The aim was to please children so they would stop him to buy ice cream and parents would place orders with the supermarket. He usually got a generous tip for it too. It was a marketing ploy that got attention from passers-by too. The Williams children enjoyed seeing him at their doorstep, as he would make them giggle. Since they had no garden, as they lived upstairs, this was open-air fun for them, and they looked forward to his visits.

On one of these visit days, Alexis was on duty at the Williamses' home, and Andreas turned up in a brown hound dog costume with long black drooping ears and a long brown tail. He handed the grocery box to Mrs. Williams with a cheerful smile, as always. While she went in, he played with the children, who pulled his tail, and he comically ran around them. They wanted to pull his ears, so he went on his knees for the younger ones. He was an amicable lad.

Alexis heard the commotion, and she came out to see what was going on. Innocent Andreas saw her in the doorway in her apron, and he winked at her with a mischievous look on his face. Alexis chuckled under her breath.

Perhaps he wasn't as innocent as he looked after all.

She broke the silence. "Come to Olynasa Pub on Saturday night. I will be there."

Alexis just wanted to be friends with him and introduce him to different people he was not accustomed to.

"Where is that?" asked Andreas.

"Near the town centre statue," replied Alexis. Andreas knew where that was.

Sunday came, and Alexis kept to her word, and so did Andreas. He was groomed neatly, and so was Alexis. Andreas was in an ironed, light-blue shirt and camel cotton trousers; Alexis wore a white summer dress with straps. Her hair was in a side ponytail held with an elastic, a red velvet flower with sequins. She wore light makeup and red lipstick that matched her hair adornment. To complete the look, she carried a red shoulder handbag and wore white matching shoes. At the pub, Andreas ordered a glass of Keo, a traditional Cypriot beer, and Alexis requested Commandaria, a sweet wine of Cyprus. And, as claimed, the wine was enjoyed greatly by Richard the Lionheart at his wedding in Limassol, Cyprus. Would a wedding take place here too?

Andreas kept Alexis amused with his adventurous stories, and he did not miss telling her about Grandma Cordelia, the elderly lady with a "trolley javelin." She was busy having a laugh and did not notice someone walking in.

In walked her admirer, the Swedish blue beret officer. He was a tall, Viking-type man in his late twenties with dark hair and a chic-casual look, with a five-o' clock shadowed beard.

Alexis was dazed. It was Sven, whom she had met at Ayia Napa before. Girls were rare in this town, so if any opportunity came for these foreign men, they would grab it. Their eyes met, and he nodded; she returned the nod. They connected. Alexis became jittery, and underneath the table, her legs were springing up and down. She couldn't think clearly. She waited to see where he was going to take a seat. A smartly dressed blond lady was sitting on her own at another table. Perhaps he had come here for her. No, he hadn't. She was the regular visitor, Marsha. The next time Alexis looked in the officer's direction, he was gone, just like ice flakes in the simmering heat. It was a quick disappearing act! Her heart sank and left a hollow feeling. She looked around to see if he had taken a seat somewhere, but he was nowhere to be seen. Andreas noticed Alexis's change of mood and inquired of her agitation, and she told him that she had just seen a man in uniform after a long time, but he was gone. She excused herself and went to look for him outside in the veranda area. He wasn't there.

Andreas did not seem to mind Alexis's search for her "genie." He did not see the Swedish officer, so he could not assist her. Alexis returned from her pursuit and settled down to continue talking to Andreas. He continued unfolding funny stories of his deliveries. Alexis had lost interest in the conversation and was waiting for Andreas to finish his drink so she could go home; she did not want to be rude to him.

Alexis was sitting facing the only entrance door, and she could see people leaving and entering. Andreas was sitting opposite Alexis. Her eyes were transfixed on that door like an eagle waiting for its prey. Then, all of a sudden, she saw her Swedish blue beret officer again! Her "genie" had returned, whisking in on a magic carpet. Her heart leapt. He had passed the doorway and was heading towards her. He had a bunch of flowers in his hand. He looked towards her and was not happy to see Alexis with a young man. He felt a tinge of jealousy.

Alexis informed Andreas nervously that her beau had come back and she hoped that he did not mind her joining him.

"Not at all," replied Andreas.

Alexis left her seat and went towards the young Swedish officer, who was walking towards her too. She had not reached Sven yet and was interrupted by an elderly lady in a "blue Monday" mood. She went for Sven's outstretched hand, which was holding a bunch of flowers.

"Are these for me?" she asked in a semiharsh tone.

"No, they are not," said the officer politely. "They are for that lady," he said, pointing to Alexis, who was coming towards him but stopped when she saw the elderly lady cutting in.

The elderly lady remarked to Alexis in an urgent, firm, growling tone, "Then *hurry up*, girl."

Alexis took the flowers and embraced Sven. The bunch of flowers had come from the florist of Hotel Saffron, which was still open due to a private function the following day, and they had extras to sell. The florist was conveniently called Handy Arrangement. This was the same hotel where Alexis had spent her first week as a student.

At the florist, Sven's shoelaces had become loose, and the cheerful middle-aged florist had pointed towards his shoes and asked him to tie them.

"Or the special delivery will not reach its destination," she teased him. Sven joined in with the laughter and bent down to fasten his laces. He raced off with his bunch of flowers towards Olynasa Pub.

Sven and Alexis went to another table. Latin American music was playing. But, unfortunately, there was no time for dancing, as the encounter had to be short. Sven had to go back to his base, and they arranged to meet again. Sven did not even finish his Carlesburg, a Cypriot beer, and left with a kiss on Alexis's cheek. He had to join the rest of his travelling team, comprising the Swedish United Nations contingency. They had to travel back to their base on the northern side. Alexis left her table carrying her glass of Othello, red Cypriot wine, and her bunch of flowers to join Andreas again.

While Sven and Alexis were getting acquainted at another table in the pub, the elderly lady headed straight for the empty seat left behind by Alexis, introduced herself to Andreas, and sat down. She did not even ask Andreas if she could sit there. Andreas froze. He recognised her. She was Grandma Cordelia, the angry elderly lady he had bugled at. She had wanted to use her trolley as a javelin. But she did not recognise him at all.

She ordered Bellapais, a product of Cyprus, a medium dry white wine with a floral bouquet and slight effervescence. She was dressed elegantly in a light-yellow, loose midi dress and black-and-yellow bead necklace. Her shoulder-length black hair was done in a bouffant style, slightly back-combed, and the front of her head was covered with a wide stretch hair band that matched her frock, giving a vintage look. She carried a black clutch handbag, and her feet were cushioned in sandals—black toe-post style with a jewelled strap. Her lips were painted in dark maroon lipstick, and there was a whiff of perfume coming from her. This was Grandma Cordelia, the elegant granny emptying her shopping trolley onto herself!

She started nattering to Andreas, giving him a summary of her historic life while she drank her wine, but Andreas was not concentrating at all until she mentioned a "Superman on a tricycle!" This got Andreas's attention quickly. It brought a quiet smile to his face, but he decided not to reveal himself to her. Instead, he pretended to be very interested in her story, widening his eyes every now and again, exclaiming "oh" at intervals, and taking a sip of his wine while quietly chuckling under his breath as she came up with her inflated version of the story. What an imp Andreas was! And what was lacking was Andreas in a colourful clown costume with cropped trousers to complement the stage acting he was into with Grandma Cordelia.

Sven left the pub, and Alexis headed back to Andreas's table. It was empty. She looked around and saw that Andreas and the elderly lady were busy having fun dancing to the upbeat Latin American music. The floor near the bar was unoccupied, so they had invaded it. High-spirited Grandma was skipping like a rabbit, and jolly Andreas was boogying as if he were on Carefree Highway, with an occasional joining of hands with Grandma and changing positions every now and again. Andreas's fear of Grandma flew out of the window. They were having fun, mingled with laughter, and so was Alexis as she watched from the audience. This is what Alexis wanted to introduce Andreas to, and she felt that her aim was achieved.

After they became exhausted from dancing, Andreas and Grandma Cordelia joined Alexis back at their table. Andreas introduced the elderly lady to Alexis with a wink, which went unnoticed by Grandma. Alexis giggled under her breath, as it reminded her of the singer Alexis T., with whom she had a mix-up at the Blue Ballantyne Hotel. She still did not know, though, that this was the lady Andreas had had a brush with.

Grandma told them that she had come to the pub to look for her husband, but she couldn't see him.

"He is spending too much time in this pub, so I came to find out what was the reason behind it," she explained.

The retired couple, English and French, were in their midsixties. They spent six months in Cyprus, inland and seaside, and the remaining months were spent between France and England, spanning over the Christmas period with their families.

But her French husband, Grandpa Pierre, was in the same building! He did not spot her. Due to loud music, he could not hear her growling voice either. He was at the opposite far end, with his back to the crowd, with a young, cheerful Filipino lady. He was a mischievous, tall, lean man with a clean-shaven face; he was in great form for his age.

Grandma was such a chatterbox that she even forgot about going home, let alone continuing her treasure hunt for her husband. Alexis wanted to bring the night to an end, as her bunch of flowers needed water. She hinted she wanted to leave and foot-nudged Andreas under the table, a sign to depart and escape. Her prediction was that Grandma would not allow Andreas to leave; she would perhaps ask him to look for her husband. But instead of foot-nudging Andreas, she accidently prodded Grandma's foot!

"Oh, my foot!" she exclaimed with a laugh and got the accidental hint instead. She said, "I better be going. I leave the night to the young ones now."

She forgot her mission to find her husband. She blanked over or didn't care about it anymore. After all, she had drunk enough. Grandma got up to leave without making any further embarrassing remarks. Andreas and Alexis escorted her to the taxi rank, and she left.

After Grandma's departure, Andreas gasped and explained to Alexis who she actually was, that she was that angry trolley lady who got disturbed by his bugle while walking on the pavement. Alexis gaped and laughed her head off. She paid her share of the pub expenses and went home in a taxi. Andreas stayed behind for another drink, hoping to befriend a young lady. A few fresh faces were around now, streaming from another pub or disco. It was getting rowdy.

It was just under midnight. Grandpa Pierre was nowhere to be seen. He left before Grandma did. His Filipino mademoiselle was still around, though, chatting with other men. Would Grandma get home before him? Yes, she did, because Grandpa Pierre had gone roaming to another pub before finally heading home after her. She asked him where he had been.

His typical fatigued reply was, "I was at Olynasa Pub, sweetie pie."

To this, Grandma said with a chuckle, "I will come with you next time, honey, but we will sit at different tables."

56

Grandma mentioned nothing of her fling at the pub. She was laughing inside her belly, and her lips quivering with giggles. Grandpa Pierre stood there wide-eyed, trying to find soothing words to coax her out of accompanying him to the pub. She wasn't going to give in. She insisted that she would escort him.

Andreas was still at the pub, bird hunting. Marsha, the smartly dressed young lady, was still in the pub. She was the one Alexis had previously thought that Sven had come for. The young lady had left the pub but returned, and she was having Aphrodite wine. She had actually come to see Michael, the chef. She was a sleek girl with her hair in a ponytail, wearing a dress in an inviting red colour, and she looked eye-catching. No men could pass her without a glance and a wink. Andreas received a positive gesture from her, and with the alcohol he had consumed, he felt bold enough to approach her and ask for a dance. She accepted. She was in a slight drunken stupor too. The end result was that around midnight, they left, swaying together arm in arm, heading for Hotel Saffron, the same one where Sven had bought the flowers. As Andreas passed the florist sign of Handy Arrangement, he thought with a broad smile that their hotel guests were opportunely arranged to be handy too!

Andreas and Marsha reached the hotel room door, and all of a sudden, he got gripped with fear. He began to scratch his head and uneasily looked around, as if he were caught in an illicit act. He politely bid her farewell with a stammer and left the hotel. On the island, being a carefree holiday destination, sex was rampant, and there was a continuous warning on the media of sexually transmitted diseases. Andreas had caught the lifesaving message. He staggered to a taxi rank and reached home without vomiting in the taxi, which had become a norm among the revellers.

Marsha had become a regular at the pub, and her relationship with Michael was flourishing. It seemed that Marsha brought good tidings to the pub for Michael. Alexis met her for a brief moment. Andreas too had become a steady visitor to the pub, and Marsha was now just his drinking companion; they laughed about their previous incident, and it was forgotten. Andreas was still a single man. Sven and Alexis saw each other regularly now.

Sven was aware that Alexis had failed her exams and was resitting them, and to fund it she was doing domestic jobs. This was common. Most of the young foreign girls on the island who would associate with a United Nations soldier would either be in a domestic, nightclub, or pub job. Sven respected Alexis for not giving up and striving to see the end result, and encouraged her to keep going. He admired her courage. And she did not discuss her domestic employers with him. Once she closed the doors of her employers, she did not take their home issues with her. She liked all of them and handled her duties through humorous eyes. She knew that it was for a temporary season.

At this stage, Sven did not talk much about his duties either. Everyone they met was scrutinised with caution, as they could be spies.

Chapter 8

What a Day! Showcase Home and the Kebab Shop

During the week, the phone rang at Alexis's place, and she answered. The continued advertisement was being well received, and she needed to carry on advertising just in case an employer dropped out. It was evening, and the call was from a lady who needed an au pair for her daughter's family in Switzerland. Mrs. Farhadi was Iranian. She inquired about Alexis's background, and Alexis informed her that she was a student waiting for her exam results. She found the phone caller friendly and the job adventurous, and Alexis jumped at temptation. Was she going to let go of everything and travel to be a modern-day Heidi on the Swiss Alps? It was not in some upgraded hut either on the Swiss Alps, but in the city of Zurich.

However, Alexis agreed to go and see her after work. She followed the road map, arrived there on time, and parked her bicycle. The white marble staircase was wide, a few steps from the street. The home had a large, black wooden door with a brass handlebar knob, giving an overall wealthy outlook. She rang the doorbell and was curtly greeted by a short, middle-aged lady, bulging big at the hips and dressed in a black midi flared dress. She showed her a seat in the hallway. It seemed dark, and Alexis had to wait for her eyes to adjust to the natural light in the room. She was thirsty from cycling, so she drank bottled water, which she carried with her, while the bulky lady settled down in her seat.

From where she was seated, Alexis could see a showcase lounge, and she realised instantly that she was not important enough for it, as it seemed Mrs. Farhadi did not hold a high esteem of her to invite her to sit in her elegant lounge. The outsized lady seemed to have an attitude that people working at the domestic level were to be handled like dirt, and they lived under her feet. But her degrading style of low treatment was waiting to be hurled back at her!

Alexis asked her what the occupation of her daughter's family in Switzerland was. She retorted that it was not her business. Yes, it was. Alexis needed to know if it was financially secure. She was educated enough from her business studies to analyse this. But Mrs. Farhadi had a monopolising plan and thought that she could control and put fear into Alexis and asked her again in a harsh and intimidating tone what she thought of the job that she had on offer. She had a mind-set that job hunters should accept her job description and salary without asking questions. She felt that she was doing a favour for them.

At this point, Alexis was fuming inside like a gas canister, ready for a sizzling explosion, and out it gushed verbally. Still seated, she gave a firm no to her job offer and gave her a verbal kick to her cerebrum, the largest thinking part of the brain, and told her to think of all people at an equal level in the future! While still seated, Alexis delivered a brisk dressing-down and cultured her on how to treat people with respect, regardless of their vocation. The potential employer remained stiff, unmoved. Arrogant Mrs. Farhadi did not want to show that the rebuking words had any effect on her, and she got up, which indicated that the door was going to open soon. Fearless, Alexis got up to leave. The maid popped her head in to see what the commotion was all about and left hastily, probably feeling justified.

As Alexis was leaving, she repeated, "Don't you ever show disrespect to anyone when your own thinking capacity is so low."

Mrs. Farhadi, portraying a superior, fearless attitude, stood on the side of the door, haughtily waving her hand repeatedly, a gesture to make her leave. Mrs. Farhadi opened the door, and Alexis passed her, turned around, and sarcastically bid her good-bye with a one-handed wave too!

Mrs. Farhadi looked at her with a plastic, unmoved face and closed the door behind her. She certainly never expected to be challenged to this extent. She sat down to get over it, and she needed something for her nerves now. She called for her maid to make *ghahveh*, a Persian spiced coffee with cardamom, served in a coffee cup and saucer with a splash of whipped cream. And she hurriedly sipped it.

Alexis cycled back feeling splendid at her feat in showing equality and justice. It reminded Alexis of the Yoga Centre, which seemed ages ago, but its information was stored away securely in the grey matter of her brain, and now she had a new addition for her "memory day" recall.

Once Alexis was outside Mrs. Farhadi's house, she felt an impulse to indulge in food due to the awful experience she'd had. The day was long, as it was summer and dusk was falling over the city. Alexis decided to stop over at Crickey Kebab Delights for a bite. The doors had faulty hinges and therefore made it tight to open. Alexis could not open it with bare hands. It would require a muscular man to open the door. As its name promised, it sure was a crickey creaking place!

Alexis parked her bicycle and stood outside the glass door, banging on it to get attention and have it opened. She even tried waving her red scarf, but to no avail. Inside, the place was buzzing with people giving their orders at the counter and taking seats. How did they get in? Nobody could hear her or took notice of her. The next eating place was a distance away, and she was hungry. Eventually, a family came out, as they could open from the inside but not from the outside. She pushed through the open door before it closed and finally got in.

Once in, she headed straight for the order counter, where a young man about her age was serving. Demetriou had short, spiked hair and wore a uniform of black trousers and white shirt; he looked neat. Half-annoyed and half-relieved that she got in, Alexis told the staff that the door could not be opened from the outside.

With a smirk on his face, he replied, "Next time, phone me from the coin box." He pointed towards the phone box that was nearby on the side of the road. "I will open the door for you."

Alexis knew that she was being wound up, so she remained calm. She had already had one adrenaline-pumping scene, and now she did not want another. She wondered for a moment if he was related to the Iranian lady? He was not.

With one hand on her hip, she responded casually, "How can I phone you when I do not even know your phone number?"

"I will give it to you," he replied.

"Okay, give it to me," Alexis challenged him. She knew he was trying to be silly with her. She waited for him as he fumbled for a pen. Instead of his phone number, he wrote on his order paper in block letters, "FREE PACKET OF POTATO CRISPS NEXT TIME YOU MANAGE TO GATE-CRASH," and gave it to her. Alexis looked at it for a moment and raised her eyebrows questioningly at him, smiling. She decided not to get annoyed. She sweetly asked him to sign and date it. He did so hastily in a boastful manner, without knowing what he was getting into; clearly, he was trying to impress her.

Alexis looked back and forth between the food credit note and him, shaking her head as if she was in a gym performing a neck exercise. She then looked at him with amusement and questioned him.

"How can I get these crisps when I cannot even get inside the cafeteria?"

"I will sit with my binoculars and look out for you."

"You are being very funny, but I will be back for my crisps," Alexis informed him and placed the voucher in her bag. Alexis actually thought that he would give her his personal phone number to encourage her to phone him, but he didn't, nor did he give the business one.

Demetriou then mellowed down and told her that the management was aware of the door problem, but it seemed that it was taking time for maintenance to resolve it. Alexis placed her order for a kebab with pieces of halloumi, a Greek cheese. She received no favours or discount. She took a seat to satisfy her hunger, and while doing so, she thought of a new name for this cafeteria.

She wrote on a serviette, in a very small font, "Clonker Delight." She went to give it to that same staff behind the counter, and comically she added with vengeance, "Get your magnifying glasses to read this, and change your business name."

He laughed, showing no effect to his feelings. Alexis finished eating and left, convinced that she would be back to exchange her voucher. She switched on her bicycle lights, as it was dark now, and cycled home with fresh air blowing in her face. What a difficult day she'd had. Traffic had died down. She reached home and slept, waiting for her next adventure.

Chapter 9

A Trip to Limassol and Exam Results

Alexis continued doing what Molly had taught her: she hitchhiked. She would hitch a lift out of the inland town of Nicosia to the seaside towns, sometimes on her free weekend, as she had an alternative Saturday off. She got a buzz from hitchhiking and loved it, and it was safe. If a man tried to thumb a lift, he would not be offered one, not even in the company of a female. Sven made no attempt, though, to join Alexis, and he was kept amused with the tales from her hitchhiking sprees.

One day, Alexis took a day trip to Limassol, a seaside town with a harbour. She hitchhiked there. Limassol was the second-largest city in Cyprus, with the largest port on this island, which was one of the busiest in the Mediterranean. The city was located on Akrotiri Bay on the island's southern coast, which had a cosmopolitan resort. To the west of the city was the Akrotiri Sovereign base, part of the British overseas territory.

Limassol had miles of sandy beaches and a vibrant nightlife, bar, and restaurants. It was the wine capital of Cyprus, best known for its red wine Commandaria. It had other varied industries, such as dressmaking, furniture, shoes, metal, electronics, and food.

Hitching a lift had become Alexis's common mode of transport. It thrilled her. On the way to Limassol, a dark blue hatchback stopped. It had an overhanging mattress tied to the roof rack and a life-sized lady sitting at the back. After settling down in the car, Alexis asked the driver, "Why are you carrying the mattress?"

He told her that it was for his mother-in-law, who was visiting them. He expressed that whenever the dear mum-in-law visited them, her mattress came too, as if he was honouring a duty of care! He said it with great enthusiasm, with eyes rolling wide and his facial muscles stretching. In one way, he was honouring his mother-in-law, as the house given to him in marriage was usually a dowry from the wife's parents. This was customary in Greek Cypriot culture; a girl's family had to be well-off to get a daughter married.

Alexis wanted to laugh at the way he conveyed it to her but kept it contained in her belly, under control. She knew too that she could get kicked out of the car if she laughed at him. After all, the extra-large mother-in-law was sitting at the back of the car, watching all her movements, ready to stop Alexis from getting too friendly with her "obedient and ideal" son-in-law. It was obviously more spacious for her there at the back than the front, where she could manoeuvre her body and stretch her arms. And no wonder the mattress was overhanging from the car rooftop. It was a king size, and all just for her! Alexis pondered, with a quiet giggle, what dowry baggage had come with his wife.

Alexis was dropped off at the roundabout corner leading to the main road on the edge of the sea. She walked down the lengthy road, and a distance into it she heard a commotion. This was going on outside one shop, and people had gathered outside. There were reporters and cameras. She turned towards the shop to see the upheaval for herself.

Was this a car accident? Was it that car with the overhanging mattress?

This was a small island, so anything of interest, however small, would get the attention of the local newspapers, as they had to sell their papers. Mr. Leon, the man from *Destiny Weekly*, was there too. He happened to be in town for business that day. She approached him, and he told her what had happened. She was relieved that it was not a car accident. The news on television that night was about shop fitters who had placed the wrong name on the exterior of the shop front. Instead of Body Bella, the graphics read Body Sensual. There was a furore about it, as this was a conservative island at the time. The older "prim and props" came out in force to stop such a shop from existing on the main road. The proprietor assured the people that the name was a "mistake" and that this was not a sex shop.

Was it a mistake? It sure got attention, and they received free advertisement for it too.

Upon reflection, Alexis decided it was clever and laughed with Mr. Leon. She told him that perhaps she should wear a banner on her back when she was cycling to advertise her home services. Mr. Leon lifted his eyebrows and chuckled. She told him that she had thumbed a lift. He did not look surprised, and neither did his moustache twitch. He was a wise man; he acquired an in-depth insight into his clients!

Alexis left the scene and headed for a swim. She relaxed on the beach, had something to eat, and hitched back in the late afternoon. This time, the car that stopped was driven by a reporter from *Destiny Weekly*; it was Mr. Leon himself. He saw her, smirked to himself, nodded his head in wonder, stopped, and asked her to get in quickly on the passenger side. She did. She was stinking from the sea salt on her body after a swim. He rolled his door windows down farther. Off he drove, allowing the air to blow in. At least she did not have to go through the well-rehearsed routine of introducing herself. Instead, she tried to get into a conversation with him, unlike other lifts, and stated that she hitched lifts for kicks to put him at ease. He noted that she was not blowing bubble gum.

He asked, "Where is your bubble factory?"

Alexis giggled and answered, feeling half-embarrassed, "Oh, I wouldn't be able to do that, as I am not sure if the driver would approve of it, and I wouldn't want to get thrown out. But I have it in my handbag. Can I? Do you know it gives a brain boost?"

Leon smiled and gave her a funny, quizzical look sideways and a tired go-ahead nod. She took out her bubble gum and began chewing. He left her to it, as he realised that it was a good way to keep her mouth occupied. Mr. Leon went silent, especially about the shop incident, as he did not wish to give away anything; he desired her to read his newspaper and tell others to do so.

The following week, the issue on the wrong signage was in *Destiny Weekly* with an apology from the Body Bella shop owners. Alexis at least had something amusing to relay to Sven the next time she talked to him by phone. Their relationship was going well and held meaning.

Mrs. Ekstrom

After some weeks, her new assignment with the Ekstrom family was due. This was for Thursday afternoons. It was a long ride to the other side of the extended town. She saw the United Nations car parked outside. They were a Scandinavian family working with the United Nations, a civil position. They enjoyed skiing on Troodos Mountain, which was not far from Nicosia; they also had a small fishing boat and spent summer weekends on the Turkish seaside. They said it was quieter there for them. They also had a fine taste for furniture and home decorations. It was a lovely home with added liveliness from their four-year-old son, Erik. On outings, Mrs. Ekstrom had her blond hair done in a topknot, dress just above knee length, and high heels to match. She was six feet tall, and looked stylish next to her equally tall, blond husband in his suit and bow tie.

Erik was a mannerly and confident child, full of Superman-style action and fantasies. His second home was his playhouse made out of a cardboard box, built for him by his dad, where he retreated for an imaginative and creative world with his mute friends—toys composed of a train set, cars, animals—and, of course, paraded in his Superman costume. He was an intelligent boy and not spoilt. He attended an English preschool nursery, and Erik was at home one day, as it was holiday. He ended up "helping" Alexis as she did her chores.

"Do you do exercise?" he asked her while she was mopping the bathroom floor.

"Yes, this is an exercise," she said mischievously. "And working with you is an exercise too." He went to ask his mother if this was true.

He returned, and Alexis gave him a twirl. He was slightly heavy. He giggled and wanted more, but Alexis was feeling dizzy and had to decline. His mum intervened and asked him to leave her to do the work. He became stroppy, and Alexis gave him another hand spin and took him to his wonderland den. She left him there to get occupied with his masks and trains. The rail tracks were laid out on the table for his toy trains. Luckily, he got busy and left Alexis to finish her work.

It was a four-hour job, which involved picking up handwoven Scandinavian carpets, vacuum cleaning, and mopping the floors. The carpets were heavy to move, and Erik would come and sit on the Hoover cylinder, giggle, and jump about. Alexis did not mind him around and played with him, tickling his tummy, which made him go into chuckling, childlike laughter. It sure did delay her work though, as there was a set job to do within the time range. She enjoyed the homey atmosphere, but it was hard work compared with others on the list. She held a view that it was better to earn a few pennies than remain idle.

"She is not going to leave a hole in your pockets, so take up the job while there is nothing to do," Michael told her. Sensible advice this time.

Alexis mentioned nothing of Sven Karlsson to Mrs. Ekstrom. She did mention this job to him on one of his irregular visits, but Sven asked no further questions just in case they turned out to be related or, worse, his boss! Alexis's mind was totally removed from exam results, and she became focussed on saving money for her visit to England after her exam results.

Babysitting Interview

Alexis received a phone call to attend to, and it set her on a babysitting quest. She could fit in these random jobs on evenings when the following mornings were free. The phone call was from a lady with a cockney accent, and she sounded like an older person; in fact, she was not, and she addressed herself as Alice. She kept on addressing Alexis as "love" and asked her if she could come round to see her at her home, which Alexis found odd. Instead, Alexis quickly suggested that they could meet at a nearby children's park at four in the afternoon the following day. Alexis gave her information on how to identify her—by her bicycle and her red bucket hat.

It was late Saturday afternoon, but days were long in summer, and it was still daylight; she cycled to her meeting point. Alexis was there at the park before the arranged time and waited for Alice under a canopy, watching the children having fun in the play area. All of a sudden, it began to drizzle, and this was the reason for a canopy, which was to be used as a rain and heat cover. On an island, if it gets too hot, the heat is followed by rain. This is because hot air rises, and it contains water vapour. At higher altitudes, it gets cool, "heavy," and condenses into clouds, and it eventually rains.

Ahead of her, outside the tall black park gates, she saw a neatly dressed woman. She wore a two-piece green suit. She was carrying a colourful umbrella and walking in her high-heeled shoes towards the entrance of the park. Alexis pondered what would happen if this lady slipped on the wet ground, not knowing that this was the same lady she was to meet!

It did not take long for her to recognise Alexis, and she came forward with a greeting. She asked Alexis if the children who were playing with the toy cars were hers. Alexis gave her an amazed look.

"No."

The woman motioned for her to go and sit down on the nearby bench. "How many children have you got?" Alexis inquired.

"I don't have any," the woman replied, fidgeting with her tight skirt.

Alexis gave her a funny look. "Then why do you need me as a babysitter?"

"I don't. I thought you needed a babysitter, according to your advertisement."

Alexis was astonished at this statement. She explained to her that she was looking for work, and her advertisement stated that.

After a bit of further discussion, it came to light that because the advertisement was placed under the WANTED column, this lady in a neat green suit thought that Alexis, who rode a bicycle and did not even own a car, wanted to employ a babysitter! This lady, Alice, could have done well in such an outfit, as a headmistress of a primary school! She completely misunderstood the advertisement, though the English language was not a problem for her. It clearly stated, "Looking for housekeeping and babysitting work." She decided to add in the future, "I am looking for…" Right now, they were presented with a dilemma of two job hunters facing each other. Alexis felt like bottle-feeding and babysitting her!

Alexis left, but not before asking her in a controlled tone that in the future she try to understand the advertisements properly. Alice was stunned and blabbered how sorry she was.

Alexis was not in a sorrowful mood. She was truly cross about what had happened, as she had had to come out in the heat and then wait in the rain to see Alice for quite some time too. Alexis rode off fuming, and once she reached her room, all her anger melted away into a barrel of laughter. She asked herself if she was even dressed up as an employer. It was Alice who looked more like an employer than an employee! What a chuckle she had over "Alice in Dizzy-land," and a tale to convey to others at the pub and, of course, to Sven, who was coming the following weekend.

Exams Results

Hot and humid days were coming to an end. It was nearing the end of August. Summer was coming to an end and so too was the flow of tourists. But the postman's work did not slow down just because the tourists did. The mailman was always needed to deliver the letters; written communication was only by letter on paper.

Alexis was in her front balcony overlooking the street, having her cup of tea. From the terrace, she witnessed the postman cycling down the road on his bicycle, which carried the letters in a large metallic basket on the front. He rang the bicycle bell to announce his arrival, riding happily down a typical downtown road that was not regularly swept, and he left letters below the doors if they were not already open due to the heat. There was a market buzz on the street, people coming in and out of one another's shops or houses, greeting each other, sometimes shouting a salutation across the road; the women's voices won the vocal race.

The postman reached the building where Alexis was standing. She leaned across the balcony to see if he left any letters for them. He did. He first had to ring the bicycle bell to make a man move from his path.

Alexis, still in her nightclothes, went downstairs to see if there was anything for her. There were some letters. One distinct envelope got her attention. It was a brown envelope with a British stamp on it.

Is this a letter from a pen pal agency? she thought. No, it was not. It had an address of the British exam board.

Her heart raced. Her blood pulsed fast. Her hands were sweating. She was having a very tense and anxious moment. She took her letters and ran upstairs to her room, making sure she did not slip on the marble staircase. Once in her room, with shaky and sweaty hands, she opened the envelope. She first went to see each individual subject that had to carry a P for pass or F for fail. The overall result had a joyous pass. She checked again. It did say pass, and she saw that each subject carried a pass too. She sighed with relief. Her shaking hands and pulse gradually went back to normal.

She felt a sense of freedom from the controls of the job market. She had another cup of tea while she pondered her business venture, before making her broadcast of her successful results. Her college was informed first. Her pub friends were joyous; her kith and kin in England celebrated with her too. After some days, Sven heard of it on the phone and promised a treat.

Alexis continued with her domestic jobs. She knew too that she would not be able get an office job so soon, and her Greek language was not so fluent. The most likely possibility would be a foreign-based company, and she did not need to apply for a visa to work.

She told her domestic employers of her exam triumph during her tea break. Mrs. Williams, the Christian missionary who was the first employer to rescue her, exclaimed in great delight with two hands clasped in prayer mode, "*Praise* the Lord. He at last turned water into wine." Alexis thought that if they prayed and water got turned into wine, then there must be barrels of wine in the Williamses' home! She squinted her eyes to this thought. Why didn't she see any, though? And she had another amused query to reflect upon. Were Mrs. Williams's kneecaps flat due to intensive kneeling for praying?

Chapter 10

A Cruise to Rhodes Island

Wilfreda painted her home, ready for the winter wear and tear; she was looking for an antichemical paint and gas masks! It was going pleasantly well at Mrs. Ekstrom's, and their son, Erik, kept filling up his fantasy den with toys. There was nothing out of the norm at Susan's farm home, except for her new frizzy hairstyle. Professor Edgar was rarely around at his place and left the key under the front doormat, as he was spending more time with his German girlfriend; she was a lecturer, as he was, teaching psychology at the same college. The only thing the German girlfriend had in common with Wilfreda was that both knew how to make a black forest cake, made with cherries, well known in Germany. Weeks went by, and it was a normal humdrum.

Sven changed the routine scene for Alexis. The promised treat was honoured. He invited Alexis on a vacation to Rhodes Island on a cruise liner, *Princess Marissa*. It was a packaged trip that included the sightseeing tours. It was nearing the end of September. They were to leave on Thursday and return on Wednesday, a sea journey taking between twenty and twenty-five hours, travelling between the two ports of Limassol and Rhodes Town. Alexis agreed and made arrangements with her employers to take time off. They were pleased that she was having a break.

Sven booked an inside cabin, inclusive of meals and excursions, and both travelled from Limassol Marina in the afternoon. Once on the cruise liner, they went on a short tour of the ship, ate in the dining room, and slept. Next morning, Friday, they had their breakfast and lazed about in

Bermuda shorts and tops, and they layered their exposed bodies with a sunscreen and an outdoor tanning lotion as they waited for Rhodes Town harbour. The sun was glowing down on the deck, which made them grab for their sunglasses. They spent their time enjoying the warm sunrays and the unending calm sea, and having amnesia of work in Cyprus!

After a while, they occupied themselves walking about the ship, checking the layout of the small cruise liner, being inquisitive, going through the small alleyways and stairs, meeting and greeting the staff, gazing at the duty-free shop, and peering in various boutiques. The vessel was massive, a fascinating, self-contained, high-rise, modern village on the sea. They arrived at their destination at the port of Rhodes Town in the late afternoon.

The ship entered Rhodes Town, welcomed by a fortress and two stone columns with a deer mounted on top of each stone column, a male and female. The legend said that in ancient times, the island had had a lot of snakes, and the deer had helped trample the snakes, so this was to commemorate the deer. But it was also said that the Colossus, one of the seven wonders of the ancient world, had stood between these two columns.

Princess Marissa anchored at the international pier right outside the walled old town of Rhodes (mentioned as city sometimes), and the private yachts and motorboats gave them a warm welcome and would give the cruise liner company for the following days it anchored. The ship was to be used as a floating hotel for those on the package tour; people left for day excursions and returned to sleep and dine, and for security, they were given an entry pass. The old town was within easy walking distance.

That same Friday afternoon, they visited Rhodes Town on foot, which was the main city of Rhodes Island. The old town was a medieval walled enclosure, and one entered through one of the eleven gates. It was officially designated a UNESCO World Heritage Site. What a thrilling bewilderment it gave them, with its maze of alleyways leading to town squares, temple ruins, and museums, and streets filled with antiquities. After a while, they wandered in a daze. There was evidence of the Ottoman Empire's rule in its architecture, with no street names to nearly two hundred streets or lanes. Getting lost was easy, but that was a delight for exotic lovebirds such as Sven and Alexis. Mosques and churches stood next to each other. The vast aroma of food flowed from the eateries serving Greek and international cuisine. From the pubs flowed alcohol and tasteful music in English, and from the taverns rang out Greek tunes. The streets were bustling with visitors strolling past tourist shops selling souvenirs and gifts for all occasions, from furniture, ceramics, rugs, leather, and jewellery to lace. It looked more like a Turkish bazaar than an ancient Greek city.

Sven and Alexis took a romantic walk down the Street of Knights, which was a long, cobbled pathway stretching from the archaeological museum to the Grandmasters Palace. They then braved a long walk up the clock tower stairs. At the top of the tower, Sven and Alexis stood there clasping their hands, taking in the engulfing panorama over the city and the turquoise sea. They visited the new Rhodes Town, which was a modernised version with upmarket shops, restaurants, pubs, and all that was familiar to a cosmopolitan city. They were tired after their walking tour of Rhodes Town. Saturday was just a few hours away, and their subsequent day plan was to go to a sandy beach.

Faliraki

There were daily bus excursions to go to other tourist sites, and the following day was to the seaside resort of Faliraki, with sandy beaches and crystal-clear water boasting water sports. They spent their Saturday in Faliraki, swimming, basking in the September Mediterranean sun getting a tan, eating grilled halloumi and lamb meat in a pitta bread at the beach, and later having a drink at a nearby restaurant. Alexis happily took photographs with her camera. But the "happy tourist expedition" was about to take a diversion.

It was time to return, and the bus was waiting to take them back to Rhodes Town to the docked ship. Alexis and Sven had gotten on the bus and settled in their seats when Alexis realised that she had left her camera on the beach bed. In an anxious and agitated voice, she told Sven what had happened, jumped out with her handbag, and notified the bus driver, Takis, a bulbous, middle-aged, bald-headed man with an unwrinkled, rounded face. He agreed to wait for only ten minutes. The beach was quite a distance away from where they were parked. One would need a long-range camera to capture the scenic view. Sven was patient, and he stayed behind with the beach bags. Alexis ran towards the beach with anxiety rising per each springing step she took. She reached the beach but could not find her beach bed, as it had been folded up. Trying to find the beach attendant at this time was going to be a task. Communication would not be so much of a strain, as Alexis was in a position to converse with him in some Greek. She turned around, and the bus was still there.

She ran to a nearby hotel and inquired about the beach attendant; he was nowhere to be found. She asked questions about her camera too—if it had been handed in—but there was no sign of it. The bus seemed far away in the distance on a hilly, snake-like, dusty road, and it was pulling out. Alexis sprinted after it and shouted to make it stop, but sadly she could not be heard. The late afternoon sun was streaming ablaze towards her eyes, which were protected by sunglasses. No matter how much she tried to stop the bus with her arms flinging like long-stemmed balloons, the coach still left her. Sven hurried frantically to the front of the bus to ask the driver to let him out, and the driver just shook his head without glancing at him. Sven then tried his military style and commanded the driver to stop the bus so he could join Alexis. He still refused, as his excuse was that it would take time to stop the bus and he had a rigid timetable to follow. The bus had to get to Rhodes Town, which took around twenty-five minutes, in time for the passengers' supper. They would first need a wash from the sea salt on their bodies and then a change of clothes—for some, into their fancy dinner attire. If the driver wanted to be reasonable, he could have stopped the bus, but he decided to be like a stubborn donkey pulling a heavy cartload that day.

Now Alexis was left stranded in Faliraki. No other transport could take her back to Rhodes Town, and a taxi was expensive. She could hitchhike, but she did not feel safe doing so at this time of the day in an unknown territory. She had only one choice now, and that was to stay in Faliraki for the night. Alexis wondered why Sven had not gotten off the bus to be with her or disembarked before the bus left. She was furious. She spoke aloud to herself, "Sven, why did you leave me alone here?"

She knocked at the low-cost guesthouses, but no room was available. The hotel rooms that were vacant were expensive, and she did not have enough money for it. She was carrying a few traveller's cheques, but they were no good without a foreign exchange office. Faliraki was unspoiled, and tourism was not yet extensive. The turnoff from the main road leading to Faliraki village was still under construction, and this was the reason why the bus had had to park so far away. Alexis felt downhearted and walked to the beach, kicking the soft white sand with her flip-flops while she thought of a solution. The sun was going down now, and she was feeling hungry. Fortunately, she had the local currency, drachmas, on her, which she used in a cafeteria to eat. She ordered a pitta bread with goat's cheese and salad. Outside the canteen, there was a donkey with an empty cart, which probably had brought in local fresh food, a harvest from the nearby fields. The only way out now was to spend her Saturday night sleeping on the beach. She had nothing warm, and the nights on the beaches did eventually get very cold on an island. She knew this from her sprees to Ayia Napa in Cyprus.

When she previously went to the cafeteria, she had passed by an open door in an old building; it was a laundry room of an adjoining hotel. She now decided to return there after she finished eating to investigate her options. The laundry room was very warm; it sweltered in the heat of the day. She recognised that this was what she would need for the nighttime: a warm room. Alexis went back to have a look at the laundry. She poked her head around, and once she saw that the way was clear, she hastily entered. She spotted a small pile of duvets, took a clean bedsheet from the drying rack, covered the duvet, and plonked on it like a tired puppy on a cushioned pet bed. She settled down to sleep, and she wondered what Sven was up to. She had no way to contact him.

Sven, in the meantime, knew that Alexis was a go-getter and that she would manage, but he was still concerned for Alexis being on her own in a strange country. His consolation was that it was a safe place. He remained calm and collected as an army man would on a battlefield; his inner military man was being tested. All he could do was pray that she would return safely and unharmed. This was a worrying situation for him, plus in an unknown territory.

Once he got to the docked ship, he showered and went to eat. At the table he was joined by a young, casual couple that had gone on a different excursion that day. They had gone to Lindos Acropolis Beach, and this was where Sven and Alexis had planned to go on Sunday, the following day.

The man was from Cyprus, and the girl was from Sweden. Both had met at a disco club in Ayia Napa, where the Swedish girl worked behind the bar. Ayia Napa was not a place for the prudish, as topless mermaids were not in shortfall, and it had become a place to go to unwind. The Swedish girl on this trip got a grand tip: a trip to Rhodes Island! Sven and the Swedish girl only had the language in common, which they used when conversing with each other. They exchanged helpful information of each other's beach trips. Sven told them of Alexis being left stranded at Faliraki Beach and that he was waiting for her return with, he added, "humorous stories of her adventure."

The couple had their meal and left. Sven felt lonely without Alexis's company and left the table. He proceeded to the bar and took a glass of Heineken onto the deck.

He was reflecting on Alexis, and all of a sudden he realised with an awful gut feeling that perhaps she had hitchhiked and something had gone wrong, maybe an accident. There was nothing he could do; the excursion bus driver was aware of her absenteeism and had alerted the ship management, but it was not within their duty to find her. He decided against complaining to the ship management of the driver's stubbornness. It would not solve his immediate problem but could add another of form filling and questions. Another option was to go to the police, but this would cause a time-consuming commotion. He opted to wait until the following day. He finished his drink and went off to sleep. There was a disco club on board, but he decided against it.

In the meantime in Faliraki, Alexis was just dozing off in her manmade, comfy, cushion bed when a maid walked in! She screeched for her to leave. Alexis jumped, and, with nothing to pack, she scurried out like a frightened rabbit before the maid got a crowd of clucking housekeepers and chambermaids together to chase her away in their shrilly voices. As Alexis left, the maid kept cursing her in Greek, which she understood, but it had zero impact on her! Alexis had become accustomed to this; she remembered how she was thrown out from the house porch in Ayia Napa in Cyprus too. While on her run to the beach, she chuckled at the thought of these two incidents. From a safe distance, she turned around and saw the same maid leaving the laundry and entering the neighbouring building, the hotel. Alexis made a 180-degree turn and accelerated her pace towards the laundry again, as if lightning were following her. She had a foxy idea! She reached the laundry room, made a dive for a clean bedsheet from the rack, and walked out quickly with it without looking back. She did not want to be a target of suspicion, so she pretended to be out strolling casually. Fortunately, no one could see or measure her panicking heart! It was nighttime, and the disco jellybeans would soon be swinging to and fro. The music had already begun to call out for them; there were young people walking about, heading to go and queue outside the disco club.

Alexis speedily went back towards the dark beach, and with the laundry room in the distance, she wrapped herself in the bedsheet from head to toe and walked in it. The beach was dark, quiet, and eerie, with only the natural light shining from the partial moon. As she walked down the beach, she looked like a Bedouin in the desert looking for water in the night! The beach beds, chairs, and parasols were folded and stacked up on the sandy beach, away from the sea. The pile of beach furniture created a wall, shaped in a square U with a space in the middle. Alexis selected this space as her sleeping quarters for the night. She began to feel frightened. In the near distance, she heard an older man guffawing, which made her feel slightly safe and that she was not alone. She was also accompanied by the constant sound of the snarling waves having their own war dance, the crests curling and landing with a crashing sound as they hit the sandy beach.

Alexis removed a beach bed from the smaller stack and placed it inside the space of the square U, surrounded by a wall of stacked-up chairs around her to keep the wind out. She did not feel completely safe, as the entrance to her temporary home was not secure from invaders. She hardly slept a wink, and the man's intermittent guffaws at least made her feel faintly secure. She kept on imagining faces peering in at the foot of her beach bed, but when she opened her eyes to look, she saw nothing and would go back to have a mild sleep again.

The early hours of morning were cold, and as morning broke out, activity began. The yapping of a puppy woke her up. It was Sunday, and most locals had their free day, and they would join in at the beach. She got up, and in the crack-of-dawn light, saw a man taking his dog out for a walk. The surface waters of the crystal blue sea were glistening under the opening sunrays, the waves laughing now and smaller, with the crests rolling gently and splashing playfully against the sandy shoreline, composing a splattering sound. Alexis's mission was first to sneak back to the laundry room and return her toga bedsheet. She folded the beach bed and left it on the side. The beach attendants would soon lay out all this furniture on the beach, and she had to be off to the laundry before she got caught again, and then return to ask the beach attendants about her camera. It was just after five in the morning, and she badly needed a cup of tea or coffee to wake up. But first, she had to take back the bedsheet. Fortunately, the laundry room was open.

She hadn't known that the laundry was open throughout the night, so she thought these people were early risers. But she could have gone back and gotten a good nap in her pet cushion bed! She went in and swiftly dropped the bedsheet in a nearby corner, and in came a maid. Thankfully, this one was a different one, and probably thought that Alexis was a night-clubbing hotel guest, coming in for a clean bedsheet.

The good-hearted maid proceeded to give her a fresh one, but Alexis refused. This left the maid perplexed. Guests came to the laundry room to "get" something, but she didn't know that Alexis had already helped herself to one. Alexis pretended to be a law-abiding hotel guest and politely made a quick exit, giving the maid a fake smile before the fiery maid of last night arrived. The maid did not speak much English, and at times like this, noncommunication was handy. She departed with hurried steps to look for a beach attendant, none of whom, sadly, had found her camera. Feeling deflated, she proceeded to the cafeteria.

Alexis set off for the canteen to have her breakfast, which would give her the energy to start her journey back to Rhodes Town and to be in time for the subsequent day excursion to Lindos Acropolis beach. It was still early for holidaymakers, but the cafeteria was open, getting ready for the holiday self-caterers, who would be arriving soon.

At the cafeteria, she asked for the price of her breakfast and a small bottle of water, and checked whether she had enough in the local currency in her handbag. She did; plus, she was given change in coins, her last in foreign currency. She had her cup of English tea, toasted bread, and halloumi cheese. With the water bottle in her handbag, she went to the hotel to see if the foreign exchange bureau had opened so she could pay for her travel back. It had not, and they informed her that it would open in two hours' time. She decided to use the waiting time to inquire at the few nearby hotels to ask whether a camera had been handed in by one of their guests. No, they had not received a camera. Regrettably, it had gone missing, and Alexis felt very disheartened, as memories were lost now. She had to accept the loss of her camera. If this were Cyprus, she would have advertised it in *Destiny Weekly* in the lost and found section, but it was not.

Chapter 11

Getting Back from Faliraki

She could not wait anymore for the foreign exchange bureau to open, and she decided to take a risk. She walked down the dusty road to the main road with the morning sun shining warmly and gently caressing her face. This was a lengthy walk, and she drank some of the water she had carried. When she reached the main road, she stood there for a while watching the cars whizzing past her. It was only around six in the morning, but already it was a busy road, complemented by a lovely early-morning sun. She waited to pick up the mental momentum and gather courage to do what her friend Molly had taught her: hitchhiking.

She stood there sticking her thumb out on the side of the road in the direction of Rhodes Town. Cars on Rhodes Island, which is part of Greece, drove on the right side, the opposite of Cyprus. Alexis had to adjust to this. Cars ignored her, as they probably thought that she had a hangover from last night's binge. She got worried, as she had to get to the ship before 9:30 a.m., when the excursion bus departed from the harbour. She persevered, sticking her thumb out for half an hour and avoiding being knocked down by the fast-moving cars. It seemed ages standing there, and she felt drained due to anxiety and lack of sleep. This time her hitchhiking was in desperation and not for fun, as it had been previously in Cyprus. Twenty minutes passed by, and then, amazingly, an open pickup truck stopped! Small pebbles flew from the edge of the road as it pulled to the side. It was an old and dusty Ford pickup truck with the aqua green paint flaking off from the side.

The pickup truck driver, a happy-faced man, in tune with the light-hearted weather, rolled the window down from the dust and flying shingles. The driver was on her side of the road because of right-hand driving.

He asked her with his pint-size knowledge of the English language, "Going where?"

"Rhodes Town," she replied with a worried look, greatly hoping that he was going there.

"Okay. We go there," he responded in a cheerful voice, motioning with his finger to get in the back. She quietly gave a sigh of relief; the air she breathed out from heaving a sigh could have blown up a mini party balloon! She was utmost grateful for it.

The truck was filled with men and women from the nearby villages, all seated, some at the front and back. There was space for one at the end of the row towards the truck's back door panel. It was a tight one for a small person, but fitting for Alexis. This was only because there were two slim people sitting in that row; if they had been larger passengers, she would have still been on the road looking for a lift. This truck was a private bus transporting people to their destination along the main road to Rhodes Town.

She had one target right now, and that was to get back before the excursion bus left for the day. She did not waste time. She went to the back of the truck and used her gymnastic skills to climb over with the help of a foothold. Due to cycling, her leg muscles were supple, so she had no problem in climbing over the truck's back door panel. An industrious gentleman held out a strong hand, assisted Alexis with her final hurdle, and showed her a seat. She was surrounded by a happy, amusing bunch.

Alexis sat down in her tight corner and could not complain because she was getting a free ride, plus they had to bear with her reeking body from swimming in the salty sea. Once settled for her journey, she drank her last drop of water. Then came the questions.

"Anglika?" One was asking in a cheery voice if she was English.

"Neh," meaning *yes*, came the slow response from Alexis.

From her corner seat, she scanned the bed of the truck and the passengers in it. They were from the age range of about thirty-five to fifty-plus, four men and two women. She began to ponder on the condition of the pickup truck. With a quiet smile, she realized that there was no need to wash this four-wheeled wagon. It was not carrying the village district governor to meet the prime minister, so why bother?

At this point, Alexis remembered Andreas, the grocery man, and his decorative cart. He would have done a grand job with such a transporting truck. She grinned at the thought of it while she absorbed the passing scenery of mountainous landscape, covered with Turkish pine trees. Her meditation was short-lived, as it was interrupted by the women next to her, all itching to delve into Alexis's personal background. They asked the usual questions while others listened: Where was she from? Where was she going? Had she stayed at the hotel at Faliraki? Was she married? They were being unsurprisingly curious, and to keep the harmony, Alexis answered their questions. Alexis told them that she had come from Cyprus and was going to Rhodes Town. She narrated the camera incident without mentioning the bedsheet, as the word was bound to get round to the hotel maids very quickly down the grapevine in this small place. The communication was a combination of broken English and Greek, miming, and hand fluttering, with some men translating along the way. Alexis mentally nicknamed her female neighbour Barrister Mole. Then came the dreaded question in a different format. Had she come alone?

"No, with a friend, and he is waiting in Rhodes Town on the ship."

Thankfully, the men joined in at the mention of the word *ship*, which stopped her being questioned further. The questionings now took a diversion. One asked which ship it was, and she told them that it was *Princess Marissa*. At the mention of this, he nodded his head calmly a couple of times up and down so as to tell Alexis that he was familiar with it. He actually worked at one of the ports where he was heading. The lady sitting next to Barrister Mole nudged her to probe Alexis about her friend who was on the ship, now anxiously waiting for her. Alexis gave her quick, short answers. It was like being interrogated in a courtroom by Barrister Mole and her clucking court clerks!

Barrister Mole had a blue triangular scarf over her head tied at the back under her hair. This matched her floral dress, covered by an apron. She carried a basket, and it was Alexis's turn to be an investigator. She peered into her basket, which sat near Alexis's legs, and could see some knitted handicrafts, lace, embroideries, and a lunchbox filled with cooked food. It looked as if she were heading for a Sunday market to sell her items. Alexis did not want to ask questions, as it would only stir a conversation when she wanted to curb it. But Barrister Mole kept her busy with her enquiries until the bus reached Ammoudes.

The truck slowed down north of Faliraki, near the village of Ammoudes, and stopped. Alexis wondered what the stop was for. It was for Barrister Mole to disembark; probably she had a stall on the sandy pebble beach of Ammoudes, which attracted multitudes because of its clear waters. The gentleman in the front opened the back door panel, and with his help, she stepped down easily.

"Yassus." She waved good-bye to all.

"Yassus," they replied. The farewells kept going on and on, and Alexis scratched her head, wondering when they would stop and allow the car to drive off and Barrister Mole to proceed with her Sunday trading. When the good-byes finally stopped, she was relieved, and she could now manoeuvre herself in a bigger seating space. She had more room now, but would she get a break for her mind to think and to relish the passing view? The truck was not speeding either; it was tailing. The road was busy with cars. However, there was a change in the volume of chatter. With Barrister Mole gone, prying lips had gone quiet.

Amid passing traffic noise, Alexis once again began to soak in the scenery as they travelled on the East Coast road that went through hilly wooded patches with the view of the sea breaking out every now and again. She spotted an occasional *dama dama* deer ready to sprint away at the noise of the truck. She wished she had her camera, as she would have taken scenic pictures.

Koskinou

The second lady broke the silence and introduced herself as Eva. She did not ask Alexis for her name; she was used to talking to tourists, and she preferred to recollect their faces rather than their names. She had a light-coloured floral scarf on her head to keep the dust out, and her hands had the rough texture of hard work. Alexis wondered if she was a kitchen maid in a hotel or eatery and if she had learned English from the tourists. In a quiet, sweet voice, Eva began to talk to her in broken English, until Alexis informed her that she understood reasonable Greek. She then became comfortable talking to Alexis in her native language, breaking out in English every now and again. She told Alexis that she lived in Koskinou and was returning from attending a christening of an extended young family in a remote village. She invited Alexis and her friend, referring to Sven, to come to her enchanting village of Koskinou. She gave her a touristic report on her home village with lots of hand movements and convincing raised eyebrows, and made it sound interesting with sparkling, storytelling eyes, as if she were acting on a play stage. She gave an awesome description of the village.

"Koskinou is a colourful, picturesque village," she said. "It is filled with whitewashed squares and charming, old, white-painted houses that have mosaic-floored courtyards filled with bright flowers. Narrow cobbled streets wind through the village in between the houses. The doors of the village houses are the most striking sight, painted in vivid colours of red, turquoise, blue, and yellow, creating distinctive mosaic colours. The doors have designs and arches engraved across the doorposts."

Alexis's ears remained propped up as Eva persisted in her fairy-like story of her beloved village.

"The new part of Koskinou is the coastal area, which has villas, fine hotels, taverns, and cafés, and it merges with the old village through a labyrinth of streets. Adults and children usually get lost in wonder in this maze of streets."

"Which is the nearest beach?" inquired Alexis, as she became more interested in the touristic information.

"Reni, which is two and a half kilometres from the village," came a quick response from Eva.

Eva began to search her hand luggage. She was looking for her confectionary box, hurrying, as they were nearing her destination, and she handed Alexis two small rectangular pieces of candy in a cellophane wrapping. It was the traditional Rhodian sweet, known as Melekouni, used at weddings and christenings.

"Please take these to your ship and give it to your friend too." She leaned over to whisper so the men in the truck would not hear her. "He will love you more, plus give you longevity." She winked at Alexis mischievously.

To this, Alexis laughed and accepted it from her generous hand. She revealed to Alexis that she owned a sweet shop in Koskinou and had made them herself.

She enlightened Alexis on the recipe, to assure her that it did not have aphrodisiac content. "Melekouni is made from our island's natural products: thyme honey, sesame seeds, almonds, orange and lemon peel, and spices," she said.

The men were busy in their own conversation, with raucous laughter booming every now and again, unmindful of the ladies' chitchat. She was astonished, as she had not thought Eva would do much talking, if any at all!

Eva was an inspiring, warm woman and a big contrast to Barrister Mole. Alexis was pleased that Barrister Mole had departed early. Alexis conveyed to Eva that she had a business start-up in mind, and the lady encouraged her to go ahead and told her that she had started young too with her husband, and they had children in the process. Alexis took a mental note that one can have a family as well as run a business.

Soon after, the truck made a throttle stop at the junction leading to Koskinou, and as Eva was getting ready to get off, she insisted that Alexis come to her charming village and gave her directions to her shop. "Come to the central village square and mention 'Eva's sweet shop' for further guidance." Eva did not forget to reference the lively nightlife to tempt Alexis.

Alexis quickly recorded this in her notebook while the men made jovial jeering noises to pressure the ladies to hurry. Eva scolded them with a good nature. There was a great camaraderie, and this is why Eva had chosen this pickup truck rather than a regular bus.

Eva did not waste time in alighting from the truck with the help of one of the men. She wanted to get to her home and business quickly, as she was the central part of both of them. She bid the other passengers farewell, and as before, the good-byes seemed never-ending, and Alexis wanted to get to her destination.

After Eva left, Alexis mulled over the information she had received and felt that the lady would certainly make an excellent tourist guide. Very likely she was familiar with giving out touristic information, as she must be doing this regularly in her shop. She also realised what a wrong judgement she had made of Eva's vocation. Alexis now had time to think things over. She once again questioned herself as to why Sven did not get off the bus to be with her. She quenched her anger towards him and wore a plastic smile for those still remaining in the truck. She had serious questions to ask Sven when she met him again.

The truck finally made its way into Rhodes Town, down the road towards the city's east coastline, and stopped near the Central Port, the pier for international traffic. Alexis did not wait for the back door panel to be opened. She leapt over it. Using the foothold, she sprang down onto the ground and felt good about touching earth once again! She waved good-bye to the remaining men sitting at the back and went to the front of the truck to give the driver her gratitude. One man got off with her carrying a duffel bag, as he worked at this same port; he was a ship repairman. Alexis bid him farewell too, and as she walked to where the *Princess Marissa* was docked, she contemplated that she might see this repairman again, perhaps fixing something on their ship. All the remaining men on the truck, including the driver, were heading for their jobs at the three different ports in Rhodes Town. The truck would be parked at one of the port's parking bays for staff.

The time was around 7:15 a.m., and Alexis hurried to the ship's entrance stairway. She was glad she was back. She showed her entry pass, and on the way to the cabin, Alexis reflected on her encounter that the jigsaw puzzle of the pickup journey had fitted well for her. Sven was not in, and the first thing she did was gulp down water from the water bottle left on the dressing table. She then saw the note, which said, "Gone for breakfast. Get ready for Lindos Beach. Waiting to hear your tales. Did you find your camera? See you soon, Sven." He had drawn a smiley face with large ears, indicating that he would do the listening!

"Oh no, you won't," she spoke sarcastically aloud to herself. "You will be answering questions, young officer."

She had a quick shower, which she needed badly, a change of clothes, and a spray of Giorgio perfume, and she rushed for the dining room carrying her handbag. She felt fresh, and she had no time to think except to rush out to the dining room to eat. She was hungry, and being on edge with her questioning thoughts did not make it easy either. They were still serving breakfast for the stragglers. She filled her tray with healthy, sustaining food and a cup of tea, which she was craving, and scoured the eating area for Sven. It was a large place, but not so massive that she shouldn't have been able to find him. She could not see him, though. Her heart sank. She went and sat at a table on her own. She was tucking into her breakfast when a hand touched her back. She turned sideways. It was Sven, jubilant and standing there. His prayers were answered.

Sven had seen her crossing the room to go to her table. Alexis was thrilled to see him, and her heart skipped a beat. However, she was cautious not to let her irate emotions run astray right now. He politely invited her to join his group at the table. Alexis picked up her breakfast tray to join Sven's team, and on the way, he informed her of the couple he was with. She thanked him for his note. This was the same couple, the man from Cyprus and the Swedish girl, he had been with the previous night.

As Alexis reached the table, and came face to face with the man, she exclaimed in joy, "Hello, you are here too!"

"Yes, I am. And this is my friend Greta," he said, introducing the Swedish girl to Alexis in great excitement. He got up to give a peck on Alexis's cheek.

He was Andreas, the man who had a grocery cart in Cyprus. It was now Alexis's turn to introduce Andreas to Sven. She explained to Sven that she had met Andreas at the home of Mrs. Williams, one of her employers, revealed how he had missed meeting Andreas at Olynasa Pub when he had brought flowers on that day, and teased Andreas that he had been busy dancing with Grandma Cordelia. Alexis spoke briefly of her stranded beach experience, her hitchhiking journey in a pickup truck, Eva's mystical and intriguing village of Koskinou, and her honey bonbon, all while concealing her anger towards Sven. They laughed at the "borrowing" of the bedsheet and the advice on the "love sweet," as she took it out from her handbag and offered it to all to taste. They liked it, and all were keen to visit Koskinou. But in all this, the sad part was that the camera had not been found. Greta did not say anything; she just giggled, as she was captivated with the hilarity of it. Both Andreas and Greta spoke positively of Lindos Acropolis Beach, which encouraged Sven and Alexis to visit this seaside attraction. And this was where Sven and Alexis were heading that day. Andreas and Greta left the table, which allowed Sven and Alexis to be alone now.

Sven noticed that Alexis's body language relayed that she was seething about something. Yes, she was smouldering with a tinge of malice in her eyes, so he questioned her with concern, "What's wrong?" Apprehensive wrinkles appeared on his forehead. She could not shout at him in public, so with controlled anger, she told him of her fretfulness that he had not managed to make the driver wait.

He informed her in a diplomatic voice that the driver had refused to stop and that even his military style command did not make him comply. Alexis looked foolishly blank at him. She did not seem convinced. Both resisted each other like an umbrella battling to open up in a heavy downpour. And, on the second round, he had an outburst.

"What did you expect me to do? Throw a tantrum and risk my reputation? He was resolute *not* to stop!" he said in a raised tone. And, due to his deep voice, it caused eyes from surrounding tables to turn towards them. It was his turn to get angry. Alexis asked him to lower his voice, or both might get thrown out of the dining room. He complied as he continued with his fruit drink.

Alexis still wanted to know why he had not jumped off with her at the time, and asked him so in a firm but reduced tone. To this, he responded in a lower, sarcastic voice and brought his face closer to hers, his breath flowing out.

"To keep the driver waiting, or he would have left." He had another sip of orange juice and continued, "And you proved that you have the determination to manage on your own." Alexis nodded at that, lifting her eyebrows in agreement.

Alexis felt ashamed that he had made an effort and apologised to him. He gave a sigh of relief. She conveyed to him how the chattering ladies had kept her mind away from and that she had been fuming over it in the truck.

She finally let it go and took out the remaining honey bonbons Eva had given her. She offered them to Sven, to revive the love between them, as Eva had said it would do. He smiled and shared it with her. The "love sweets" certainly did the job!

Then Sven questioned her, with a mischievous edge, "Was there place for me on the truck?"

"No," came the reply, and *this* was an eye-opener for Alexis. With no extra place, they would have been separated, as it was.

Alexis finished her Sunday breakfast and both left the table, as Alexis had to go to the foreign exchange bureau to cash her traveller's cheques so she could buy a camera from the ship's duty-free shop. Alexis wanted a camera with a neck strap and a name tag so she wouldn't lose it. She purchased one with the film cartridges that were required to take photographs, and a hand strap came with it. She hoped that it would be difficult for this one to go missing.

Sven had another starry-eyed plan to charm Alexis, after what had happened. He asked her to select a piece of Rhodian jewellery she liked. She selected a silver pendant with a deer as a central design. Alexis appreciated this kind gesture and leaned across to give him a kiss on the cheek. She decided to return this thoughtful gesture at their next destination.

Chapter 12

East Coast Boat Trip

The lovebirds made their way to the cabin to get ready to leave for Lindos Beach, their next destination. They carried water bottles and energy drinks purchased from the dining hall café. While on their way out, they saw an advertisement in the passageway that read that there was a one-day boat cruise from a nearby harbour of Mandraki along the East Coast. It read that it was sailing to Lindos and going past the bay of Anthony Quinn, named after the well-known American actor and for his filming of *The Guns of Navarone*, a war film, in 1961. Sven looked at his watch; there was still time to catch the boat trip, which was leaving at 9:00 a.m. He discussed it with Alexis, and she could not agree fully to it, as she was concerned about how they would get back from Lindos, after her stranded experience at Faliraki. Sven suggested they go and suss it out more first, from the booking office. They quickly rushed to their room, carried their prepared trip rucksacks, and packed their drinks, camera, and its cartridges.

They hurried to the harbour, and they were in time for the boat cruise aboard the *Kalypso* (sea nymph in Greek mythology). The receptionist at the booking office eagerly informed them of the schedule.

Alexis still preferred the coach trip to Lindos, but Sven wanted the boat cruise. They debated back and forth for a while. The thirtyish female receptionist was intrigued. She had dark hair done in a ponytail held upwards at the back, looking like a Christmas tree with hair accessories on it. And on her nose sat squared, black-framed glasses, which magnified her eyeballs. She raised her eyebrows, widening her eyes, and tilted her head in the direction of whomever was speaking as she followed their argument intently from left to right, like a policeman's torch hunting in the dark; she was getting a neck massage on the job!

When she had had enough of the neck actions, she reached under her desk, brought out a whistle, and blew like a train guard to stop the squabbling. Sven and Alexis stopped abruptly, a bit shocked, and with wide eyes, they waited eagerly for her master solution. The receptionist convincingly gave them a plan to cruise by boat and link up at Lindos with the coach trip organised by the cruise ship.

"I know Takis, one of the drivers," she commented in her Greek accent, with a wink, and laughed. This was the same driver who'd left Alexis at Faliraki. She continued with a touch of glee, "You are better off giving him a rest, if he is on duty."

Alexis had the ship's organised coach schedule in her handbag and examined it. The timings fit, and the well-informed receptionist was not wrong. Alexis finally agreed to take a boat trip, and Sven gave a sigh of relief. The receptionist also assured them that they would have enough time to go to Lindos Acropolis and tour Lindos, if they did not spend too much time drinking at the beach.

They bought their tickets, and then Sven asked the receptionist if she used the whistle often.

The receptionist chuckled. "Yes, regularly, to wake up the afternoon passengers in the waiting room as they doze off." She quickly added with a serious face, "And yes, also to stop arguments." The morning sunrays smiled with them as they embarked the boat.

At the same time, a rough-looking man also purchased a ticket and boarded with them. He was a tall, muscular man with rugged features and shoulder-length hair. He wore sunglasses with a Panama cowboy hat and rough denims. His name was Iakob (Jacob), and he carried a rucksack. In it were a few shirts, wigs, sunglasses, his jail uniform, and a replica gun. He was carrying disguises, as he was on the run from the police, who were after him.

He hurriedly brushed past them and nodded a "Hello," which Alexis returned with a mumble.

The boat left Mandraki harbour, sailing down the east coastline with a considerable number of people on board, cruising at a leisurely pace to enable sightseeing. Alexis and Sven now had the opportunity to view the coastline from the sea; previously it was from the roads. The small two-tiered cruise boat, painted in blue and white squares, had a matching overhead cover, used against sun and as a shelter against rain. The boat was open at the sides to allow for fresh air and sightseeing from the benches. The guide talked to the passengers through a red megaphone and made an announcement to introduce himself; his name was Daniel.

They enjoyed the tranquil scenery, passing sandy beaches and small inland villages covered with rugged olive trees with the guide's voice in the background. Alexis checked to see who was around. Iakob took a deck chair upstairs away from the crowd who were more eager to see the coastline passing by. He had no interest in sightseeing. He kept his distance away. The guide was too busy to even notice or question him. They always had people from all walks of life, so this nontourist approach was not unusual.

Alexis and Sven became curious and since they had already had a brief encounter with him, they approached him to have a conversation. He did speak some English. He told them that he was a hotel chef on a break. This was a lie. He had a different agenda.

If he could do one thing, he would become invisible at the sight of the police and become visible again to enjoy his earthly gain, stored away in a secret location. He had robbed a wealthy couple of their jewellery from a hotel. He had been in jail for his crime but escaped with inside help by being carried away in a wheelbarrow, sealed in a box labelled "potatoes."

A small elderly lady on Sven and Alexis's deck kept on screeching at the sight of anything moving or static on land. An elderly gentleman of the same height who shared her passion of excitement accompanied her. Both had wrinkle-free faces and wore matching clothing. They both sported red Bermuda shorts, white T-shirts, and red baseball caps, bringing vibrancy to their age. Both carried cameras and lightweight binoculars around their necks.

"*Look!*" she screamed at the sight of a deer, which ran off just as fast as her scream came out of her mouth.

Deer do not need hearing aids! They have sensitive ears. This one probably heard her shrilly voice and decided to make a quick getaway just in case it became a target for a barbeque for these sea wanderers. All those around on board jumped and turned to look in the direction of the sprinting deer; it spoiled their mood of concentration and tranquillity.

The boat sailed through to Kalithea Beach, close to Faliraki. The guide informed them that this was famous for its medicinal hot springs, spas, and scuba diving. It was a place with palm and pine trees and buildings influenced by Arabic architecture.

The beach cliffs stood against clear green waters, creating tiny coves and inlets where locals enjoyed coming for a swim. The elderly couple aboard wanted a slice of the idyllic scenery, so they came to where Alexis and Sven were seated on the crowded side facing the coastline. The woman squeezed them apart to take pictures. The elderly lady was thin and robust, and her husband craned his neck over her shoulders from behind. Alexis and Sven looked at each other and giggled, and she felt like pinching the elderly lady's bony legs to make her squeal, but she decided against it. Instead, Sven and Alexis both seized the opportunity to enjoy the serene scenery and take pictures, even though they were confined to a limited space.

Once they went past the beach, the older lady struck a chord with Sven and began to talk to him. At such times, Alexis had trained herself to be a smiling mannequin! She was feeling sleepy but overcame her tiredness with a dose of vitamins and an energy drink. The older lady told them that she and her husband were from Italy, and they were here to see if the island was suitable for them to retire. Alexis propped up her ears and decided to open her dummy mouth. She informed the Italian elderly lady of what Eva from the pickup truck had told her of the magical village of Koskinou, an option they could consider, perhaps, for retirement. She showed interest, took note of the name, and asked Alexis its location.

"We just passed it," Alexis told her.

The elderly lady, Bianca, moved away to allow the husband to take her place as she went to the guide to inquire about Koskinou. Her husband, Alberto, got busy. He began conversing with Sven, at the same time gazing through his binoculars and taking memorable pictures. Alberto and Bianca were a lively and talkative couple who had been journalists in their working years.

The boat continued with its journey. In sight was Ammoudes Beach, and Alexis waved good-bye to Barrister Mole as she told Sven of her encounter with her and her interrogations. Sven came out of his quiet self and made a comment in a funny, female-like accent. "You should have told her that I swear to tell the truth, the whole truth, and nothing but the truth, and what is your next question?" They laughed aloud, which made Alberto and Bianca turn around in synchronism, and what a comical sight it created, of two pairs of protruding binoculars and red Bermuda shorts, focusing on them! This made Alexis and Sven chortle more.

The announcement came through the megaphone that they were soon to sail through the quiet nudist/naturist beach on the way to Anthony Quinn Beach. This got most people's attention and made them chuckle. The mature men gave quiet inner smiles. It was an undisturbed and remote beach, appropriately surrounded by trees. Sven teased Alexis that he wanted to get off here and bond with nature. Alexis chuckled, knowing that he was joking.

On the boat, Alberto and Bianca got into their gladiator action with their binoculars glued to their eyes, laughing and providing an expressive commentary to those who had to rely on their naked eyes to see. In their passionate Italian accent and with humour, their art of journalistic observations flooded the nearby crowd in turn:

"A man has covered his private parts with a *pointed* Mexican sombrero to prevent it from getting sunburnt!" Bianca paused for a while for a private giggle.

"Mama mia, there is a woman walking about with a short white veil on her head." Alberto chuckled. Comments rolled on, and their voices became more excited.

"A man seemed to have arrived wearing only an apron and a cook's hat," he said.

Bianca exclaimed, "*Santa cielo*, mama mia! There is an artist at work with his canvas on an easel, sitting under a sun umbrella. How can he concentrate?"

Eventually, with dullness in his voice, Alberto revealed to the listeners with a chuckle, "Do you know, instead, it is more beautiful to watch the background scenery of the seashore and the hilly wooded areas than the Adams and Eves on the shore?"

This banter was translated to a nearby small group of lively young adults by their sign language instructor, Ionna; they were on an excursion from Cyprus. The young hard-of-hearing group went into a roar of cackles, and some clapped their hands in excitement. It brought a smile to those watching the aftermath. Ionna was assisted by a responsible male supporter. She looked very summer-like in her white, flowing, soft, cotton midi skirt and pink cheesecloth top. Of course, she also had sunglasses and a straw hat.

Bianca added with a glitter of amusement, "A naked tree is only good for a log of fire." The stand-up comedy took off well again, but, conveniently, the sign language instructor did not hear this. Amusing remarks continued until the boat sailed past the beach. Some were interested in visiting the place in their own time and made enquiries with the boat guide.

Alexis's concentration for a moment wandered to Cyprus and to Grandma Cordelia and Grandpa Pierre. How would they have reacted to a naturist beach? Grandpa Pierre would have certainly enjoyed it, and his wife—well, if she could become a wolf, she would have made the nudists scuttle from the beach.

Anthony Quinn Bay

The next stop was the chocolate-box view of Anthony Quinn Bay in Ladiko, flanked by two cliffs. Surprise was waiting for all.

Everyone was looking forward to disembarking here for a swim or walkabout. The small cruise boat *Kalypso* moored at the jetty, and they were given thirty minutes to stretch their legs. Daniel, the guide, asked the passengers to stay within easy reach to hear his whistle for a roundup.

The bay was most suitable for snorkelling, but there was no time for it. The beach water was emerald green, surrounded by lush green vegetation; the shoreline was covered with sand and pebbles, with rocks in and out of the waters, making it unsuitable for swimming for the elderly and the children. The water was slightly colder now than it was in July and August. However, Alexis and Sven dipped in for a swim, the young hearing-impaired group splashed about, making a joyful noise at the shallow end, and their newfound friends, Alberto and Bianca, opted for a stroll and later slumped in the folding chairs on the beach, which allowed their zooming binoculars to have a short break. Instead, they found some Italians on the beach to unleash their adventures to; this was a popular beach for young Italians.

Thirty-five minutes later, the cruise guide gave a final whistle, and the boat drifted out of the bay towards Lindos. The sea was calm, and the sun was gleaming warm. The boat sailed lazily. Bright and breezy staff came out with refreshment trays and drinks. They wore white knee-length shorts, white blouses for the ladies and shirts for the men, and dark blue baseball caps. Alexis asked for coffee to stay awake and had a salad and sandwich to eat. Sven had the same.

The next sighting was a pirates' village. Daniel's broadcast got eyes peering towards the coastline as they got nearer to Afantou (or Afandou). This was one of the oldest and largest village of Rhodes Island with less-developed beaches, and it was perfect for kids. Afantou could boast that it was the only village on the island that had an eighteen-hole golf course, overlooking the sea.

Sven and Alexis were content with their boat excursion but wished they had brought two pairs of binoculars from Cyprus to enable them to see more clearly.

Afantou meant *invisible*. The reason was that in the past, the villagers did not want their village, which was strategically placed behind a hill, to be seen by the pirates plundering the Mediterranean island, and this is why it became known as the pirates' village. Today, it was a bustling village, and a miniature train brought people from Afandou's main square, shuttling visitors between the village and the beach.

The boat cruised on to Tsambika (or Tsampika) Beach, a long, broad beach with fine, deep-golden sand, dotted with canteens. The beach had a shallow, emerald, crystal-clear coastline that made it ideal for families with children and allowed space for beach games. It was also suitable for water sports, and a hilly wooded area surrounded the beach. The boat went into a hove-to position so people could have a good look at the beach and its surroundings. The commentary was addressed over the loudspeaker, and the sign language instructor took her position in front of her small group to interpret it to them.

"Tsambika Beach gets its name from the monastery above the hill there." The guide pointed towards a jutting, steep hill in the distance, overlooking the beach. Alberto and Bianca aimed their binoculars in that direction and allowed Alexis and Sven to view it, while others queued for it too. He continued, "From the hill, the view is breathtaking, as far as Lindos. It has no village here but only a seaside."

"Can people get up to the top of the hill?" asked a passenger as the rest followed the gaze to the hills.

"Yes. The car will only take you halfway up the hill, and then you have to walk up the dirt tracks and pine trees to the bottom of the monastery. Then you climb lots of steps leading to the church itself. It is a long journey and not for the weak."

"Oh, I would not be able to climb that," exclaimed Bianca.

"Yes, you would, if I were a kangaroo," came a joking, quiet reply from her husband. "I would carry you in my pouch."

This made Alexis and Sven smile with a very quiet giggle, so as not to offend the romantic Italian couple.

The guide continued. "The legend says that it works miracles for childless women when they come to pray here. When the child is born, they name it Tsambika, after the monastery."

The commentary resumed with a light chortle. "The island is full of these names—Tsambiko for a boy, and Tsambika for a girl. Just ask for these names on a busy street on the island, and you will soon find out how busy the monastery has been!"

Everyone laughed at this as the boat cruised past Tsambika Beach and the hills to the next stage of the journey.

The talk on children named after Tsambika Monastery resulted in an inner awakening for Sven. Sven wanted a family of his own, and he went quiet, his thoughts drifting into a faraway distance. Alexis, on the other hand, was still recovering from her exam results, and "breeding" was not on her mind. She wanted to first visit Britain before deciding on what to do next: stay or leave. Alexis had to nudge Sven to come back to the present day and to get his attention. She pointed to the passing village, as the guide commented upon it.

It was the village of Archangelos, popular for the art of ceramic pottery, carpet making, and wood-fired, oven-baked bread. The traditional houses were wholly beautiful, painted in vivid colours, and arches and walls were decorated in ceramic plates. The ruined walls of a medieval castle overlooked the village.

From the *Kalypso* cruise boat came the jolly laughter of the passengers as a banana boat ride whizzed past them, towed by a powerboat. They were nearing Stegna Beach. It had long stretches of white sand and catered mainly to those who were particularly looking for a quiet and secluded place. There were no bustling shops or nightlife, but in some areas, fish taverns, cafés, and bars could be found; it was not commercialised.

Suddenly, the banana boat made a sharp turn to purposely tip the five tourist riders, both young and older. They fell off, laughing. The hard-of-hearing adults on the cruise boat held their breath as they saw them tumbling off and were relieved to see that the riders were safe. The banana riders were floating in the water, as they were wearing life jackets, and were in full swing, entertaining themselves. The rest on the *Kalypso* joined in watching the amusement, and peals of laughter rang out. Around them were other water sports such as paragliding, snorkelling, and water skiing.

St. Paul's Bay and Lindos

The boat sailed past Stegna Beach and continued its serene journey along the east coast. The boat finally reached the rocky bay of St. Paul's Bay at Lindos, and there was a loud cheer as it moored at the jetty. They would have a whole afternoon to wander around St. Paul's Bay, Lindos, and the acropolis. St. Paul's Bay was another picturesque location with deep, blue, clear waters and with delightful manmade and natural rocky and sandy beaches, which could be a bit stony for bare feet. The bay was a cove enclosed by hills and overlooked by the medieval Lindos Acropolis, situated on the stately hill. Alexis and Sven parted company from the tired-looking Italian couple, who must have exhausted their eyes from binocular watching, and waved good-bye to the excited young hearing-impaired group, who were in a hurry to get off but refrained by their leaders as a precautionary measure.

On one side of the bay on the hillside was a charming white chapel of St. Paul, named after the Apostle Paul, as he was shipwrecked near Lindos on his way to Ephesus and took shelter there. It had a large courtyard with magnificent views of the bay, and there was bunting hanging from the rails of the church piazza, and a violin playing for a wedding that was in progress. Sven and Alexis went "bride watching," and they danced a short ballroom on the side of the large church courtyard. This chapel had become an ideal place for tourist couples to come to for their dream wedding in an idyllic setting. Would this entice Sven and Alexis to tie the knot here too?

Iakob was on the police's "Wanted" list, and they were on his trail. They had a tip-off that Iakob was heading by boat towards Lindos, where his ex-wife was living. The police from the Lindos area were checking all cruise boats.

Here at St Paul's Bay, the uniformed men were waiting! The policemen of Rhodes Island were waiting to search the *Kalypso*.

Iakob quickly put on a long blond wig and changed his sunglasses to circular vintage ones. The police boarded the boat and examined each face while looking at the photograph they carried. The runaway villain just gazed at the scenery as if it did not bother him. But it did. His heart was pounding as they scanned his face back and forth, up and down, and eyeballed the photograph and him, several times. In the end, they took him for a nutty tourist. Iakob was relieved and sweating. He stayed on deck, and smoked a cigarette.

"If you are looking for someone, try the nudist beach," commented Bianca. Sven and Alexis chortled. But the police were serious faced.

They tried another technique. They came for another round and showed the "Wanted Man's" photograph to the passengers, but they shook their heads from side to side with sad-looking fish pouts. They went back to the disguised Iakob. He did the confused "yes-no-maybe" headshake, the Indian subcontinent style, from side to side and up and down, giving a muddled message. The frustrated police suspected that he knew something. They took hold of his shoulders and shook him fiercely in anticipation that he would tell them where the runaway was! As he realised that he was going to be led off and his blond wig might fall off, Iakob shouted, "No, no, no." The police threw their hands angrily to their sides for "wasting their time" and left him. He made a false disgruntled sound, and once they were out of his sight, he grinned to himself at how he had fooled them.

Iakob made a quick exit. He went for a walk to the chapel, which had memories for him. He met Alexis and Sven outside the church, and he enlightened them about his chapel wedding, which they listened to with great interest. Then, Sven asked him where his wife was. He answered with a tinge of regret that she had left him. They did not probe further.

He removed his hat and went inside the chapel to reminiscence about his marriage to a girl from Lindos. He would love to turn the clock back and live a simple life. Greed had destroyed him.

From St. Paul's Chapel, Sven and Alexis set off hand in hand for a ten- to fifteen-minute walk uphill and then down to the Lindos Village centre. Lindos was built on the sides of a steep hill, and because the roads were narrow and difficult, it was traffic-free. Strong legs were needed to tour the place. But what a stunning view of Lindos, if those legs could carry you. If they couldn't carry you, you could hire a donkey. The dazzling white traditional houses sat beautifully tiered on a hillside, down to level ground. The city had cobbled streets and alleyways, and Lindos Acropolis overlooked the view from its hilltop fortress position.

Their plan was to tour Lindos and the acropolis and go back to Rhodes Town by their ship's excursion bus. They had to find someone from the cruise ship to help them find the bus. For this, they headed to Pallas Beach, located in a cove beneath Lindos Village.

They spotted someone with an umbrella that had *Princess Marissa* printed on it in bold letters, and by his side was a bottle of Hellenic beer, Mythos, half-buried in the sand to keep it cool. He, in a semidrunken stupor, informed them that the bus was to leave from the car park, uphill above the village, at 5:00 p.m. He pointed in its direction. They were pleased to know they had time to tour the village, but quickly realised that they could not be sure this man was a passenger of *Princess Marissa,* so they scoured the beach to find another person, and they did. He was none other than the no-nonsense, timely bus driver, Takis, the same one who had left Alexis behind at Faliraki. He was used to dealing with rowdy young tourists and had a stiff approach towards them.

Takis recognised Sven and Alexis from the Faliraki trip and sniggered. Sven, who was still captivated with the beauty of the village, came out of his quiet corner and asked Takis from where and when the bus was to leave. He gave them the same information as the tipsy man had. He pointed towards the car park in the distance above the village on the hill.

"From there, Krana main car park, at five o'clock," he commanded in his strong Greek accent.

"Apharisto," replied Sven in his Swedish accent, thanking Takis in Greek.

"And don't be late again," the driver hollered after them, ending with a chuckle.

They all laughed. At least they had made harmony with the disciplinarian driver.

He continued, "Look for a bus that has a board on its front window with *Princess Marissa* written on it. Have your ship pass ready too."

Sven and Alexis left him to enjoy his basking, and probably ducking and diving for a hidden beer in his rucksack to evade his passengers seeing him.

By now, they were hungry and found a beach tavern, where they had lunch of lamb *moussaka*, a recipe made from eggplant, lamb, and cheese, *tzatziki*, which is cucumber-yoghurt dip, and the red wine, Silenus Red, which was much appreciated. The tavern overlooked the sea with the Lindos Acropolis towering above it. From looking at it, Sven and Alexis knew that after their meal, they would surely need energy to get to the top of the acropolis.

Acropolis

At the summit of the hill soared the ruins of the acropolis of Lindos, another fortified castle. Lindos was traffic-free, and the only transport available for tourists was the donkey taxi. Alexis and Sven hired a donkey ride, which consisted of two donkeys yoked to each other. They rode off from the donkey station near the town square and up the steep gradient on an uneven gravel track to the ancient ruins. The donkeys knew jolly well where to travel. The fast-moving donkeys trotted past pedestrians, weaved through the narrow track, overcame humps and bumps, and at times narrowly missed dangerous drops on the side that had no safety railings.

In the hurrying process, the donkey nearly threw Alexis off her seat, but she held on to her seat grips, giving a nervous laugh to ease the fearful throbbing in her stomach. The striking surrounding views helped her get her mind off her phobia. Sven, on the other hand, was revelling in the "clippity-clop" ride, although his legs were slightly long for the stirrups. But this did not bother him.

All that could be heard in such a serene environment was the trotting hooves of the donkeys, the crunching sound of the gravel, and the donkeys braying. The peaceful and tranquil atmosphere, the heat of the sun, and the great views had a mesmerising effect on both Alexis and Sven. They finally reached the end of their ride, and it took them around fifteen minutes to get to the ground level of the acropolis. Alexis gave both of the nongrumbling animals a rub on their backs as they were left to have a rest in the shade with sufficient water to drink from their master's staff. She jokingly named her male donkey Hurricane Tsambiko!

On reaching the bottom of the ruins, they now had to walk up a lengthy flight of steps that led to the top of the acropolis. The water and energy drinks they carried were most convenient, but a breathtaking view awaited them, and this was to make it all worthwhile—the view of the surrounding harbours and coastline with stunning St. Paul's Bay on one side and beautiful Lindos village on the other. Alexis and Sven stood there clutching each other's hands. The silent atmosphere with such an exquisite view was overwhelming for Sven; he turned to kiss his *flickvän*, meaning girlfriend in Swedish.

While fondling Alexis's hand, Sven related a funny army episode he had encountered.

"I and my workmate were on a patrol, and we saw a figure in no-man's-land." Alexis looked at him with eager eyes to give a cue to continue.

"We drove towards it in our army jeep across the grassy land, untouched for years, bumping along protruding rocks. He was a herdsman and spoke Turkish and a bit of broken English. He had strayed off for greener grass for his herd of goats.

"The herdsman was tall and thin, in black trousers, white shirt, and a white chequered cloth on his head held down with a rope-like band, like a Bedouin, to give him shade from the sun and dust.

"I went forward while my mate kept a watch, and in Turkish I greeted him, '*Merhaba.*' And he replied back in a throaty voice, '*Merhaba.*' I explained to him with lots of hand signs and broken English that he has to move back to official land and showed him with my hand where that was. He understood what I meant, and he moaned for a while, and then he related to his goats by bleating to them. '*Baahhh, baahhh.*'"

Alexis laughed at the way Sven imitated bleating sounds.

Sven continued, "And the goats responded back. It seemed the goats got the message that they had to go. I then decided to communicate with the goats too, and I bleated at them. But oddly, the goats did not respond back."

"What happened then?" asked Alexis curiously, as she was interested in the other side.

Sven replied, "The herdsman laughed loudly in his husky voice. He explained in mime language that the goats recognised his voice and not mine. I and my colleague were amused. This was a learning curve for us."

Alexis chuckled, and so did Sven.

He continued, "With that, the herdsman rounded up his goats using his long stick and talking to them. We helped him round up the animals, which required a special technique. Phew. The herdsman was led back to authorised land and he waved good-bye at us."

Sven nudged at Alexis and added, "Do you know that goats have excellent night vision and will often browse at night if not securely locked in? They are intelligent animals and can learn to open gate latches." That was animal knowledge for her. She hardly saw animals where she lived in Britain or Cyprus.

After twenty-five minutes, they finished touring the acropolis site and made their way down by foot following the donkeys. On their exit down, they met women selling lace, cloth, and similar items and wondered if Barrister Mole was among them. *Perhaps her items may have ended up here through a sales chain!* Alexis looked around for her with a giggle, but she was nowhere. She just wondered with a mischievous smile what pins and needles she would have probed Sven with to get information out of him.

On their saunter down the donkey route, she told Sven of the rest of her adventure from Faliraki in the pickup truck, which made their stroll humorous. This was to compensate for navigating the slippery stones, avoiding colliding with the donkeys, and treading into their poo.

Alexis teased him, "Barrister Mole may have coaxed you to join a dating agency."

"Yeah, a dating agency called Donkey Yokes," he added quickly in jest. They chortled, and without warning, Sven had to leap over a blob of donkey poo to avoid plodding his feet into it.

At each level going downhill from the acropolis, the spectacular scenery of Lindos below was magnified as the village got closer. They did not miss out on taking photos either, and also asked a passer-by to take theirs together.

All of a sudden, Alexis felt a stinging itch on her toe. She looked at it, and there was a large, angry blister along the edge of her left toe. It was sore! And, to add to this misery, her legs began to ache like a throbbing tooth. It dampened her mood immensely. Sven, with a military physique, was not immune to tempers either. He became irritable. Both were tired now.

"Where are we going now?" he asked in an edgy voice.

"Beach!" Alexis responded back in the same tone.

Their walking trail finally brought them down to Pallas Beach, and they dumped their rucksack on the beach without speaking to each other, changed into swimwear, and rented the sun beds. They disagreed over the choice of drinks. Alexis told him in a touchy tone to get his own, and she would get hers, herself, later. She was in pain. The sun was still shining hot in the afternoon.

He settled for the local beer and returned to find Alexis had gone for a swim. She headed straight for the water to cool off and heal her sores in salty seawater. Sea salt is anti-inflammatory and antibiotic. Apple cider vinegar or pure aloe vera gel would have performed the healing trick too. Sven decided to leave Alexis alone, and he could see her swimming in the distance. He needed space to think.

Alexis returned, dried herself, and left to buy a drink, remaining mute the entire time. When she returned with her glass of drink, Sven had gone. *He threw salt in the wound.* She scoured the seawater, but he was nowhere to be seen. Sven had gone far away towards the deep end to aqua massage his deflated mood to make it work like a turbine again. Alexis shrugged off her concern for Sven and craned her neck to look at her blisters, which had gone down, helped by her healthy immune system too. She needed space as well, and closed her eyes to enjoy the sun and think while lying on the sun bed.

They did not have the whole day here, and time was limited. It seemed a long rest when Alexis felt a man standing next to her. It was Sven, drenched in water and wiping dry. He took his drink and said, "Cheers."

She in return lifted her toe and said, "Cheers." She turned on her side towards him and sipped her drink. That brought a smile to Sven's face, and he bent to touch her foot to look at the blister, which was calming down. The dead skin was wrinkling over it.

She turned on her stomach and asked Sven to massage her back. Ooohh, it felt good; those firm hands oiling her creaking bones, and the beer played its role too. They had a lingering kiss, and it was time to leave their short afternoon swim. They then realised that both had bought the same drink—Mythos served in frosted glasses—and yet they had initially argued over the choice of the drink!

In return, Sven also wanted a back massage. Her tender fingers went up and down his spine, leaving a tingling feeling, and he was about to doze off when Alexis lightheartedly spanked his bottom to wake him up.

They quickly changed into their clothes, and Alexis walked barefoot and carried her sandals, and Sven transported her rucksack. Once on the cruise ship, she would seek medical attention.

On the way out, they bought two chocolate crepes, one for each. These creperies lined the beach; they were not in short supply. They travelled on foot to take a look around the village. They still had time for it before the bus left for Rhodes. Sven also had time for revenge—to dab Alexis's nose with the crepe's chocolate sauce. She tried to do the same, but she could not reach his nose. They giggled and joked as they toured the village

Lindos was a fairy-tale place, quaint and beautiful. The architectural character of Lindos Village was a mixture of Roman, Byzantine Greek, Italian, and Turkish. It had a labyrinth of narrow, cobbled streets, bustling with a bazaar of tempting gift shops, pubs, cafés, restaurants, and taverns with Greek music playing in some.

The houses had impressive wooden doors that led to hibiscus- and bougainvillea-filled courtyards, layered with black-and-white pebble mosaics known as *kokklaki*. The doorways here had distinctive stonework, like ship cables or chains, to represent the number of ships the owner had possessed. These were the historic captains' mansions, with decorative gateways, now either rented out or used as restaurants.

Sven had a wristwatch with an alarm, so he set it for half an hour early, at 4:45 p.m. They did not want to be left behind. Some tourists were using a donkey taxi. The donkeys were taking visitors around the village with a guide, and Sven and Alexis had to meander away from them to avoid bumping into them. They passed through a maze of narrow streets, up the dainty staircase, and then down another street lined with whitewashed buildings and shops.

Alexis saw Sven was busy peering in a shop, so she grabbed this chance to buy him a gift from another kiosk. She selected leather sandals, told the shopkeeper that it was a gift, and showed him Sven, whose back was turned to them, to ask him if they would fit him. She went up to Sven and asked him to try the handcrafted sandals.

"What for?" Sven asked.

"So you become a crusader saint," Alexis replied mischievously.

He laughed and added, as he tried the sandals, "And grow long hair and a long beard, wear a long robe, and dare wink at a woman!"

The sandals did not fit him, and they exchanged them for a larger size. Sven showed his appreciation by squeezing Alexis's hand, leaning forward to kiss her forehead, and whispering, "I love you." She exchanged her love through body language. He placed the sandals in his rucksack, and they continued their walkabout. He was still carrying Alexis's bag.

Alexis was feeling tired now and was thankful when Sven's wrist alarm went off. They immediately turned their attention to *Krana* car park. Yes, they found the bus with the name tag in the front, and the driver was already seated behind the wheel, with few passengers already seated. He opened the door and let them in. The bus tour guide was nowhere to be seen yet. Was he the semidrunken man they had met under the *Princess Marissa* umbrella?

They also had company. The police van was in waiting too nearby. Iakob was being led away with different-coloured wigs hanging from his rucksack. Alexis and Sven were stunned. They approached him to find out what was going on, and he revealed in shame what he had done. He realised that gathering wealth in honesty lasts long.

The police had found him in the chapel, and when they showed him the photograph, he removed his wig and told them the image was of him. He gave himself in and revealed the secret location of the loot.

Alexis immediately slumped off to sleep in her coach seat. She left it to Sven to keep an eye on their belongings. The guide came back looking relaxed and cheerful, and he greeted weary passengers as he checked the passes of those already seated and those arriving. He was that same man who had been under the umbrella, a different guide from the previous day. After the beach splash, the bus guide they had seen on the beach went visiting his restaurant friends, had a meal, and followed it by a siesta in the courtyard at the back of the eatery. He was sober enough to drive, though. He also knew that there was always another day for him for swimming and sunbathing; his tipple came first! The bus left on time, and all the seats were filled up. The bus driver had surely driven home a message to arrive on time. It took around one hour from Lindos to the harbour where the cruise ship was anchored.

On arrival to the floating hotel, they went for supper and returned to their cabin. Alexis was exhausted, and she was for once very grateful for her bed and bedsheets. She slumped off to sleep, and so did Sven. There was still one more day on Rhodes Island before they returned to Cyprus.

Chapter 13

West Coast Coach Trip

The Cyprus conflict was ongoing news on Rhodes Island, which is part of Greece.

Back in Cyprus, talks for peace between the two sides kept enduring but to no avail, as the Turkish occupied side wanted their occupied state to be recognised, and the Greeks obviously refused. It was only acknowledged by Turkey; no other international governments accepted it. And the word *peace* was only on paper. The Greek Cypriots refused a face-to-face dialogue with the opposite side.

Bad news broadcasted, but the planned West Coast trip on Rhodes Island was not involved in the political row and therefore was to continue.

The following morning, Monday, was the final day on the excursion bus, and they left on time, as they had to be back to get ready for departure the next day. The coach trip was taking the passengers to the West Coast to see the Valley of Butterflies, the wine-producing village of Embona, and then across to the East Coast to see the Seven Springs.

The stern-looking driver, Takis, was well groomed and wearing a neat, ironed shirt. He seemed to do a great job as long as he was cautious and concentrated on the roads. At least he did not have to haggle for a living; he just had to drive tourists around, and he could sunbathe during working hours! What more could he ask for?

Today's guide was a different one from the previous day; he was Stephanos, a young man, and he too arrived looking fresh. He was in his jolly self and livened up the atmosphere. The first thing he did was test the microphone for the commentary. The sunrays streamed through the glass windows, giving passengers a glowing, carefree feeling. Most became adrift in their own thoughts. It was a warm, sunny day, but there was a possibility of rain pouring, according to the time of the year.

The bus was only partially full, and this meant singles could sit on their own rather than sitting in silence next to an odd fidgety one. They left Rhodes Town and headed towards the West Coast. This side of the Rhodes coastline was more agricultural than the East Coast, as the winds predominantly blew from the west. This made the scenery greener than the East Coast. The West Coast beaches were unspoilt, quieter, and less crowded than their sister coast counterparts.

Valley of Butterflies

They passed several villages and the airport. Twenty minutes later, they came to Theologos (Thalos). Nearby was a shaded green valley, the Valley of Butterflies (*Petaloudes*, in Greek). The guide allowed the passengers forty-five minutes to tour with him and stop for coffee or sightsee on their own. While the tourists wandered around, Takis went for a date with his Greek coffee to catch up on the local news at a cafeteria inside the valley. Coffee to him meant delighting his five senses; he communed with it with Aphrodite's language of love! Firstly, his eyes met the gaze of the coffee cup. Then his hands fondled the cup handle. He sniffed the coffee, followed by a loud "aahh" to show satisfaction. He sipped it noisily, and finally, he treasured the memory of a splendid taste! To him it was like ordering and tasting a missus! If you were going to be delayed for his bus, this was the time to ask him for a favour to wait for you. He would have another cup! After all, brewed coffee increased longevity; he desired to drive the bus for many more years, well into his seventies.

The Valley of Butterflies had a creek that was blue-green in colour from the reflection of the Oriental sweet gum trees and the surrounding green vegetation. It was a beautiful forest in a valley with scenic cascading waterfalls, the rhythmic waters waltzing down the small, steep cliff to dine with its companions below, the serene ponds laid with graceful water lilies and hidden aquatic plants. It was flattered by a pretty wooden footbridge with crisscross-patterned wood railings. The valley had shaded, narrow, pebbled walking paths, and rugged, slippery stone steps led to an uphill walk to the monastery.

The area was scented, adding to the charm; the storax resin secreted by the trees created a strong vanilla scent. Together with the coolness of the valley, both of these conditions attracted millions of butterflies during the summer to fly to the valley to reproduce. The Jersey tiger moths were camouflaged as they rested against the tree trunks, stones, cave walls, and board signs. This made a fascinating sight to a butterfly lover, especially when they flew and different colours became alive. But it also left tourists confused or angry due to the signs getting covered up.

Since Alexis was not one of these butterfly admirers and was not in a mood for it, she separated from the group and wandered off on her own to appreciate the beauty and silence of the valley. She came back and joined Sven to tell him that she was venturing to see the outside scenery; she was not in a mood to be with the crowd.

Outside the Valley of Butterflies, while Alexis walked around and glanced at the hilly scenery, she mulled over the beautiful valley scenery inside. This landscape could make an attractive painting or print on a plate.

After a bit of sunshine and walkabout, she strolled back inside and drifted to the souvenir shops at the entrance of the valley, where she saw in front of her what she was meditating on: prints of the butterfly and valley landscape on a plastic plate. She bought two decorative plates with a butterfly print on them and wandered about on her own. There was a newspaper stand selling the English version of the local paper, and she purchased one. She found a seat to read. In it was an article that got her attention: "Nicosia in Cyprus plagued by a rapist."

The next line read, "A masked man was targeting lone women walking about at night in the upcoming area of Nicosia."

Here, there were grass fields ready for development. Police were on high alert and so were the warnings to the public. This was very odd, as Cyprus was relatively safe and civilised. Alexis was alarmed, as she often travelled on her bike in the early hours from her babysitting rounds. All she had faced so far was a drunken man making noises as she whizzed past him, because her bicycle presence had scared him. She was already feeling downhearted, and this was not going to help.

While the police were trying to uncover this crime mystery, Alexis and Sven were on their soul-searching journey on a different island. A sighting of familiar faces in the distance elevated her mood.

A few other excursion coaches from various parts of the island were there too. From among one crowd, Sven, who was still with the group, heard a familiar voice. It was Alberto and Bianca, the Italian couple. They became excited upon seeing Sven but contained themselves, as they had been asked beforehand to be silent due to the sensitive butterflies, so the three of them waved at each other until they ambled together to the cafeteria, where Bianca asked with a quizzical face, "Where is your butterfly?"

"I have not selected a favourite colour yet," replied Sven naively.

"She means the two-legged lady and not the two-winged one," chortled her husband.

"Oh, you mean Alexis?" Sven exclaimed, embarrassed.

"Yes."

"She went outside. She had a glance around and seems to prefer the outdoor scene instead." Gratefully, they did not probe anymore.

In the vicinity of the cafeteria, Alberto and Bianca told Sven that they were going for a day's trip the following day to Symi, a nearby Greek island, from Mandraki harbour in Rhodes Town.

The following day, midafternoon, Sven and Alexis were leaving for Cyprus, or they would have joined the Italian couple and visited Symi too. Sven could see his guide, Stephanos, leading people out, so he concluded his conversation with the Italian couple and made his way to the coach. Takis was already behind the wheel, and Alexis was seated in the coach. Once Sven settled in the bus, she showed him her two purchased printed plates—one was for herself and another was for her first employer, Mrs.

Williams back in Cyprus—and the newspaper article. He scratched his neck as he read it. He did not know how to react to this.

He had noticed that Alexis was feeling low, and such an article was not going to elevate the mood. He told her of his encounter with Alberto and Bianca and hoped that this would cheer her up. It did lightly, and she updated him that she had seen them from a distance. Sven told her of what was discussed and that she was referred to as a "butterfly" and pointed his muscular finger at the butterfly print on the plate. Alexis raised her eyebrows and laughed quietly. She was gradually coming out of her gloom.

Sven educated her that the sweet aroma of the resin from the trees was used in the perfume industry and to manufacture incense. Alexis listened with great interest to the rest of Sven's knowledge on the valley, gained from the guide.

He continued. "Alberto and Bianca wore matching blue Bermuda shorts and blue-printed shirts, and, yes, they had their binoculars too."

He chuckled as he resumed, "If the duo ever got detached, they could easily be paired together again with no difficulty at all. No spoken language would be needed!" Alexis cackled so loudly that it turned a few heads around. At least, the bus driver knew that she was not late! Also, Sven had managed to revive Alexis to her normal self again.

Embona

The coach was ready to go to its next destination, the mountainous and inland village of Embona, where they would be tasting wine and getting a flavour of Greek folklore.

They followed a winding road through pine and cypress woods until the smell of grapes engulfed them, and this was a sign that they were entering the village of Embona, the wine centre of Rhodes. The coach stopped for the free tasting of a variety of locally produced wines at the largest winery. They had an opportunity to buy wine bottles, and Sven bought two bottles of red wine to take to his army base, and Alexis bought two wine bottles; these were sweet white dessert wines, one for Michael and another for her landlord.

The crowd gathered near the bus, waiting for their guide to arrive. Stephanos returned and in a loud voice informed them of the locally produced, pure distilled spirit *souma* as the passengers boarded, and the driver arrived too, carrying a bottle of sparkling wine. The guide enlightened them that *souma* was strong and got one drunk without the drinker realising it.

He continued with his commentary. "In a hectic situation, one shot of *souma* will relax you and allow you to face any difficulty with a smile!"

The driver grinned and nodded his head in agreement with the guide, as he himself secretly kept a bottle of *souma* in the bus for tense days, and so did the guide. They took their positions in the driver's and passenger's seats respectively and winked at each other. Both searched their rucksacks for *souma*, and each took a sip!

Both the guide and the driver beamed, showing just what *souma* would do for a person. The guide turned his head around so that passengers could hear him, and added with humour, "Souma is an express solution to stress!" The passengers and Takis chuckled. The driver took them to the village of Embona without a further sip of *souma*!

Embona was situated at the foothills of the island's highest mountain, therefore making it the topmost village on the island. It was completely unspoiled by tourism. The village was full of life throughout the year and renowned for its inhabitants' dance skills. Many still wore Greek local costumes to keep the traditions alive.

The passengers got off the bus and were asked by the guide to meet at the village centre and stay in the vicinity to hear his whistle blow. They meandered around the tranquil country village with the sound of crickets chirping in the background and the air blowing with a gentle waft of oregano and sage, from the cooking of local meat dishes. Village houses had colourful painted gates, and some were overhanging with homemade rugs and other handicrafts for sale.

At the village centre, the village's local women, dressed in colourful Greek costumes, were performing a traditional dance. They held hands and formed a semicircle with two men dancing in the middle. The inhabitants of Embona were of Cretan origin, so their songs and the dances strongly reflected those of Crete.

The swarm of tourists who had descended on Embona in different coaches were being entertained by the Embona dance group. Alexis looked around to see if Alberto and Bianca, the Italian couple, were around. She could not see them, but alas, their other old friends from the East Coast boat trip were around. Alexis noted Ionna, the sign instructor, and her hard-of-hearing group with the male assistant hovering in the background. The young adults showed their boundless enthusiasm by complementing the dance with raucous clapping. Ionna spotted Sven and Alexis too and waved at them, but the tourist crowd was quite thick for them to walk through to meet each other.

The local bystanders, old happy-faced females, were waving their handkerchiefs while the Greek dancing and music were underway, and there was no plate smashing to avoid injuries. The young hearing-impaired adults caught the gist of it and began to wave too; they flapped their caps, and some males took their T-shirts off to wave about violently, as if they were in a Spanish bull-fighting ring. This surely attracted the dancing group's attention. One young girl came forward as the rest of her dancing group took a break and asked the excited hard-of-hearing group to form an arm-to-arm line so she could teach them to dance through action. There was mayhem! Laughter peeled through the air. They were like a group of jolly Jo-Jo clowns, and people loved them. Soon, the Greek dancing team returned, and it resumed, and the cheerful "silent" bunch returned to their seats. They at least had recharged a few human batteries as well as theirs, and many would have queued up for it daily at a battery station, if such was available for an upload!

Stephanos, the guide for Sven and Alexis's group, blew the whistle and escorted them to a tavern to devour lunch on an usual sunny day; people were hungry and thirsty. Sven and Alexis ordered a bottle of water, an alcoholic drink, Ouzo, to go with the *meze*, and *paidakia*. grilled lamb chops with lemon, oregano, salt, and pepper. Once they satisfied their appetite, they all set off again, the entire group, each with a purchased bottle of water.

The coach stopped at the village petrol station to fill up the tank. They then proceeded to the back of the village. At a spot down the dirt track, the passengers got off the bus to view the remote islands of Symi, Halki, and other surrounding islands.

Sven pointed to the small island of Symi in the distance, as guided by Stephanos, and conveyed to Alexis that this was where Alberto and Bianca would be heading the following day. He added, "If we had time, we would have gone there too. It has been said that it is a colourful and pretty mountainous island, which only takes an hour by ferry from Rhodes."

The guide supplemented the rest of the information. "Symi has a very beautiful harbour, with notable tiered triangular-roofed houses on both sides of the steep-sided fiords, some in white and some in pastel yellow. However, most beaches can only be accessed by water taxis from the town. If you want to enjoy tranquillity, this is the place to go to."

At such a time, both Sven and Alexis desperately wished for the presence of Alberto and Bianca for their binoculars. To buy a pair, they would have to venture out into Rhodes's cosmopolitan town, and due to their hectic programme, they could not schedule this.

Seven Springs

They departed to go to the Seven Springs. The trip was across to the East Coast while their lunch digested, and they waited to reach Seven Springs.

The guide gave them an hour to tour the place, as they could better grasp it when sightseeing than when listening to a commentary. The guide grabbed the opportunity to head for a Mythos beer bottle at a tavern and put his feet up to rest on a nearby tree stump, accompanied by the driver.

The valley had seven sparkling springs, which gushed all year round into a creek and flowed into a river leading to a manmade lake. The place had a romantic Mediterranean touch to it; it was surrounded by woodlands and a bubbling stream trilling gratifyingly. The river flowed under wooden bridges, which carried poised ducks and geese. Birds chirped and proud peacocks strutted on the walking trails leading to the lake. The place offered an idyllic atmosphere.

To add excitement, there was a dark tunnel with shallow, fast-flowing water. Sven and Alexis removed their walking shoes and waded through the dim tunnel. It took them around ten minutes before they saw sunshine again at the other end, near the plains of the lakeside. They came out holding hands, grateful to see the sunny day again.

After walking around, Sven and Alexis were happy to stop at a tavern for a drink. This was amid the woodland near the river. Humans made slurping sounds of beer in the heat while peacocks, geese, ducks, and birds made their "voices" heard too. Sven had Heineken beer, and Alexis had a glass of fresh orange juice.

Both were absorbed in the silence of the unperturbed attractiveness of the place. They were in their own thoughts, as their journey together was coming to an end. Their friendship had matured on this Rhodes passage, but where was it leading to? The unspoiled idyllic setting of Seven Springs reminded Alexis of the romantic setting of the Chinese Willow Pattern story of a runaway couple, which was painted on the white-and-blue Willow dinner sets sold in the high streets. She looked at her watch and nudged Sven lightly to come back from his faraway thoughts. Sven was a very reflective man.

"It is time to get back to the bus," she said gently.

They saw the passengers from the same group leaving and made their way, following the crowd, hand in hand in silence.

The Russian Couple

The coach drove back to the agricultural West Coast by going around the mountainous forest, which contained the Valley of Butterflies. The bus slipped away from the entrance of the valley, continued past the airport village of Paradisi, and was on its route to Rhodes Town.

As Cyprus was locked in and out of the peace talks, another war was being fought on another continent. It was between Afghanistan and Russia, the largest country in the world.

On this bus route back, Sven and Alexis ended up sitting across the aisle from a middle-aged Russian couple. The man had wide shoulders and a calm, even smile. She was slight and lean and held her head high with her long, graceful neck. He was casually dressed in dark brown shorts and white T-shirt and wore leather sandals. His wife was dressed in a plain yellow dress and orthopaedic leather sandals, with a leather handbag swinging from her shoulders. She wore two hair plaits neatly lined in opposite directions at the back of her head. Sven, sitting on the outside of the aisle, noticed that the Russian man next to him kept on bringing out a chained pocket watch. He would open the case and give a "ballerina tap" on it, and out flowed patriotic music. It was the Russian national anthem; this appeared to gladden his heart and kept him in touch with his motherland, Russia.

Russia was at war with Afghanistan, and there were uprisings within the states of old Russia (Union of Soviet Socialist Republics, or USSR) due to the poor shape of their economies. (This eventually led to its dissolution into fifteen independent countries.)

The couple were the fortunate ones living abroad in France; he was a watchmaker, and his wife was a ballet teacher. They had two children with them, a boy aged eight and a girl aged six, and they sat in front of their parents. They were neatly dressed with sun hats. Brother and sister were jumping and playing teasingly with each other. They were oblivious of what was going on with their parents behind them. The father's behaviour seemed normal to them. The mother kept on peering over the seat to tell them in Russian to look outside to see "this and that" scenery. She surely had a handful in her care.

He took a swig of vodka, wiped his lips with a handkerchief, placed the capped bottle back into his knapsack, and looked at his wife with a delighted expression of sheer fulfilment that could not match even his wife's company! The bitter wine, vodka, was a jewel of Russia. She smiled gently at him, as a devoted wife would. Sven turned towards Alexis and whispered with a giggle, "I wonder if he will even remember his wife's name at the end of the journey."

The Russian man spun sideways towards Sven, and for a moment Sven thought that he had heard his remark. No, he had not, and instead he asked Sven for the time! Sven was puzzled, as he had seen him entertaining himself with his timepiece. As if reading his mind, he casually leaned across the aisle towards Sven and told him that the music on his pocket watch was working, but presently the time had been erratic.

With vodka slowly taking effect on his mind, he added zestfully, "It is not a kind of watch that would be given to an American president, hey, unless he wants it for a vintage collection." He leaned backwards on his seat and laughed heartily, and Sven could not help chuckling either. Sven informed him of the time, which was afternoon now. After thanking him, the Russian watchmaker turned towards his wife to join her silent gaze. She was concentrating on the passing scenery, perhaps to make her forget the turmoil in her home country while she fanned off the heat. Sven and Alexis gazed from their window until they reached the harbour.

They arrived at the cruise ship, which was waiting for them in the harbour. They were all tired now. The passengers said their thanks and farewells to the lethargic driver, still in his seat, as he performed a nodding head ritual as each one left. He was also aware that another tourist group was in the pipeline after his day off the following day. He was certainly looking forward to his rest time, to his sparkling wine, and to having a break to tame his nodding neck!

What type of crowd would be next? Would he need *Souma* to relax and put on a plastic smile? The present bus group of mixed ages had been better behaved. There were times he had a group that was unruly and was glad to bid them farewell. He also recollected with a smile that he had left gutsy Alexis behind; at least she had managed to return to Rhodes Town. But, if he only knew how she had done it, it could require an oxygen mask to resuscitate him, as her hitchhiking tactics would be a novelty to him.

Everyone clambered up the ship's stairway to reach their cabins to have a rest and get ready for supper. They were in good time for it. The Russian couple staunchly walked up the stairway arm in arm, locked at the elbow. The dutiful wife was holding tight to her husband to protect him from falling off and making a spectacle of himself. The children looked tired and followed them obediently, and the boy held on to a bag of souvenirs.

As soon as the husband reached his bed, he plodded right onto it; vodka had taken over and veered him onto its own route. This was the reason why he could not read the time on his pocket watch!

Cruise Ship Departs from Rhodes

Sven and Alexis packed up and went for a stroll on the deck. They were quietly appreciating the brisk nighttime breeze until they bumped into Andreas and his new girlfriend, Greta. They cheered up the atmosphere and made Sven and Alexis forget that the memorable journey had come to an end. They drank, chatted, and laughed at each other's adventures until bedtime.

Andreas made them chuckle by the manner in which he related the bugle and trolley incident with Grandma Cordelia and described how he had escaped her fury. Greta, in her two pigtails, was now ready to talk rather than be a listener, and in her near-squeal pitch, she told them of her piggyback ride from Andreas while coming down from the acropolis and how both had come tumbling down, laughingly. If they were pigs, the farmer would have sold them off fast, as they would have been costly to keep!

The following day, they waited for the ship to cruise out of port. The horn blasted around midafternoon to let everyone know that they were officially underway, and it sailed out, leaving behind the port's heritage castle wall and the two columns of deer and stag. Alexis and Sven both stood at the deck rail in a tranquil mood and observed the ship sail out of the harbour and slowly cruise away from Old Rhodes Town. The tides and weather were calm, and the sun was still out.

As the cruise ship sailed out farther into the Mediterranean Sea, it started to get chilly as the winds picked up. The winds and waves at intervals lashed angrily against the portholes, and the ship was now on its own, surrounded by a vast sea of blue waters, sometimes calm and at times agitated. Sven and Alexis were positioned at the deck rail, looking romantically in each other's eyes. They kissed as a sign to say good-bye to Rhodes. She added a whisper of thank you to Sven as a mark of appreciation and finally said, "I love you." They both left the deck, hand in hand, and went to their cabin with their rucksacks and their gift bag containing the presents and souvenirs covered in a towel to cushion it. They had a shower and a change of clothes for supper.

In the dining room, they were looking forward to meeting up with their acquaintances Andreas and Greta again. Andreas popped in hurriedly to carry food back for them and give them the bad news. Unfortunately, Greta had taken ill. She was having a bout of seasickness, a type of motion sickness also known as kinetosis; the symptoms were dizziness, fatigue, and nausea. Andreas told them that the ship doctor had come round to see Greta, and he had recommended cyclizine or ginger, and she had selected ginger root, as it had no side effects.

"Capsules or candied ginger cubes?" the doctor had asked.

The doctor provided her with the capsules and his favourite item— the medical bill.

Andreas lightheartedly confided to them that when she slept, Greta made high-pitched squeaky sounds when she exhaled. Andreas was fortunate not to get the dizziness, as the long-term use of the silicone earplugs could cause it too. It was a choice between risking giddiness and his brain hearing squeaky noises! He did not want to suffer sleeplessness. Andreas questioned if there was an alternative solution to curb snoring, as antisnoring sleeping aids had not worked.

"Drink no wine four to five hours before bedtime," mentioned Sven.

"Are you serious?" probed Andreas.

"Yes, and it works. At least, it has for some," replied Sven.

"Then I will pass on the information to the snoring Greta," said Andreas, laughing inwardly, as Greta loved wine before bedtime. He made his way to collect food for the two of them.

It was Alexis's turn to go silent as she listened to Andreas, and they decided to join him to go see Greta. She was lying down. They hung around for a while until it was time for them to leave for their own cabin, waiting for the day to end to do their final packing for their departure after breakfast.

Chapter 14

Back in Cyprus from Rhodes Island

Back to Army Life

The next afternoon, the ship sailed into Limassol port in Cyprus. Sven and Alexis joined the queue with their passports and ship's passes and so did Greta and Andreas. Greta managed to walk on her own, slowly, though; the remedies for dizziness and nausea had worked, and her strength was picking up with energy drinks.

At the customs entry barrier, the stern customs officer asked Sven and Alexis if they had anything to declare officially, and Alexis professed with humour, "Oh, yes, leave your high heels and take your binoculars instead!"

The uniformed customs official did not see the funny side of it and asked again if they possessed anything of high value. Sven, stifling laughter, showed their unused traveller's cheques, wine bottles, camera, gifts, and souvenirs they had brought in. The customs official was now suspicious of the giggling tourists, so he checked the rest of the luggage in detail, including the pockets. He found nothing to confiscate and asked more questions on what they were doing in Cyprus and for a proof of residency, which they both produced. Sven and Alexis stopped tittering now, as they realised how serious it was getting. After some interrogation, the customs officer finally let them into Cyprus with a welcoming smile; his mood had changed swiftly.

It had been a refreshing holiday, but they were not greeted with sunny weather; it was a dreary day. The clouds were darkening, with heavy rain in the air. Sven had to get back to his base in Famagusta, and Alexis back to Nicosia. They travelled by taxi to Larnaca, where they were to part after their pause in the waiting room for their taxis in different directions.

The announcement for Alexis's taxi bound for Nicosia came. Sven lightly gripped her shoulders, squeezed them to encourage her to pull herself together, and kissed her lightly on her left cheek. Both approached the shuttle taxi to Nicosia.

"It reminds me of the trip in the pickup truck from Faliraki, when I got left behind," she commented to Sven as she boarded her taxi, squeezing into her seat. Sven smiled when he saw a thin lady getting in from the opposite side with a bucket covered with a thick, white kitchen towel, towing in an odour of fish. She was wearing a black scarf tied under her hair and a plain black frock; she was a widow. She had just bought a quantity of saltwater fish from a fishmonger, and some were still alive and flapping about, creating a swishing noise at intervals. She settled her blue bucket in her lap, sitting at the other end of the taxi from Alexis. The waft of fish smell spread in the taxi; some began to pinch their noses with handkerchiefs or tissues. The fish-keeper was on her way to her village, catching her transport connection from Nicosia to her village; probably she owned a fish restaurant in or near her village.

Fish was expensive in Cyprus; it was considered a speciality dish. Cypriot fish were mostly grown in local fish farms or came from the seas around Cyprus. Imported fish was fresh and came from certain approved fish farms from around the world.

The taxi was still being loaded with passengers and goods for the car boot, and Sven waited for the taxi to depart. The weather was getting more dismal but not pouring yet, just rumblings in the sky. One well-dressed, skinny man with a briefcase was grumbling over the fish. He was worried about his suit absorbing the fish odour.

Sven was standing near Alexis's window and mused with laughter, *It will be oven-baked fish at some place tonight, and the grumpy man should make enquiries of it instead of complaining. He might just get invited to a sizeable meal out of kindness. He needs it!* Sven scratched his head as an afterthought.

The taxi started its engine, and Sven waved Alexis good-bye and shouted, "I will phone you." The taxi left.

Sven's plan was to travel by a private taxi from Larnaca to the checkpoint crossing and then walk across the buffer zone of northern Cyprus, occupied by the Turks, and hire another taxi to his Famagusta base. Ongoing trouble was brewing between the two sides of Cyprus, so it was tense at the Green Line. The locals did not even want to mention the other side, Turks or Greeks. The situation was edgy. Sven's and Alexis's individual destinations were both less than an hour from Larnaca.

It began to drizzle. A man in his youthful years, small in build and height, walked into the taxi waiting room with an overcoat over his head to protect him from getting wet. His destination was Famagusta too. This small man in civilian clothes was from the same United Nations base as Sven, and they knew each other. They cheerfully shook hands and agreed to share a taxi. They informed the taxi office of it, and both sat down inside the waiting room and chatted. Outside, it was raining now, and it seemed it would be some time before their taxi departed, but at least Sven had company. His soldier friend told him that he had come to Larnaca for the *naughty* girls. This was common practice, so nothing new for any trooper to hear of this. The soldier friend chuckled as he elaborated on the girls and the visits he had made, and all Sven could do was give a stretched smile. He had made up his mind to settle down now, so frolicking was out of his range.

Sven told his companion of his trip to Rhodes and encouraged him to visit the "magical place," as he called it. Sven was hungry and went to a nearby snack stall to purchase a doner kebab and a can of Carlsberg beer. His friend followed him too, as he was starving; these romping girls were not there to cook a dinner for him!

The taxi arrived, ready to take the soldiers to the Famagusta crossing. Rain had stopped, but it was bound to start again. They travelled in a more comfortable style than Alexis did. The Larnaca taxi only took them up to the Greek speaking side of the dividing line. At the crossing, their identity documents were checked. They walked across the Green Line and took another taxi from the Turkish occupied side to take them to the Famagusta military base for the Swedes. They both had to be on duty the following day, so Sven went to sleep early, ready to be up the next day, mentally and physically alert for his army orders.

Sven was on military staff, and only a few were still in Cyprus under the direction of the United Nations.

Back in Cyprus, the momentum was building up; the search for the rapist was mounting and everyone was talking about it. Police were on high alert and so were the warnings to the public. This was very odd, as the island was relatively safe and civilised. Alexis was alarmed, as she often travelled on her bike in the early hours from her babysitting rounds.

Alexis's landlord checked on his female tenants and warned them of the rapist, if they were still unaware, as he collected the rents. He knew that Alexis had been away.

The police had a description of the body and build of the rapist, but not of his face yet, as he kept his shiny mask on during his ordeal. He spoke in a local accent. They had taken swabs for DNA from the victims, but no match had been found. The police decided to set a trap for him.

The rapist knew of this massive hunt, as he glued his face to the television, which only came on at nights. It gave him thrills that he could not be caught.

The rapist story had stalled. The police were on edge—where or when was he going to strike again? The police chief got worried and asked questions. *Was the rapist informed of the police setup? How? Was there a spy in his operation, working with the rapist? Or was the rapist a policeman himself?*

The police were not going to give up on their search and decided to use behavioural psychology aimed at the criminal mind, hoping that it was not one of their men. They sent a false television broadcast, asking a "lone woman" seen in the upmarket suburb not to wander around at night. She was no other than the protected female policewoman. It was a sting operation.

The plan worked. The rapist got caught. They removed the mask to see his face. Unknown to Alexis, she had met this man! A shocking revelation was awaiting her.

When Alexis reached her flat, it was dark already, and she turned on the television to listen to the news. There it was—the broadcast revealing that the rapist had been caught and was in prison awaiting trial.

And then they showed his face. She stood there and gaped! He was the affluent George who had lived abroad. She had met him behind the Trixos Building for a job interview in a Mercedes-Benz car. She gasped and thought, *What a lucky escape I had!* She kept on shaking her head in disbelief for a while. She did walk out on him, though, but felt at the time that he was "civilised" enough not to have forced anything upon her, and how wrong she was.

Sven's Peacekeeping Duties

At Famagusta, the peace keeping soldiers were assigned to observation posts. This was a life of patrolling in light armoured cars, looking through binoculars, or making rounds with the trained sniffer dogs. The tasks were menial, and on the whole, it was quiet on both sides. What they had to look out for was in the no-man's-land, for unauthorised construction, poachers, or strayed farmers and herdsmen. Both sides of Cyprus had generally respected the ceasefire and the military state of affairs, social or political. The blue beret boys in boots maintained the peace, too.

It was late afternoon Friday, and Sven was on duty with a comrade. They heard firing sounds, *rat-tat-tat*. Immediately they got into action to investigate.

In the distance, they saw a crowd had gathered, and as they got closer, they found out that it was a slingshot contest. Using a catapult and a stone, one would aim at a tin hanging from a pole, and the queue of locals moved fast. The crowd jeered or cheered.

The locals asked Sven and his comrade to join in, and they did. It was a chance to show them what well-trained marksmen they were. The crowd gave loud applause at their military might. They left the locals to enjoy their day.

They had another episode. It was mid-October and getting ready for winter. Hay was getting transferred to the barns for the animals, either from storage or newly purchased. Sven and his workmate were once again on a patrol, and ahead of them was a cart pulled by a donkey. A normal-size man with a moustache, wearing red trousers and a red Fez hat, was manning the reins, making the donkey work, while he whistled away since the trot was slow.

In the United Nations patrol car, Sven was driving, and the vibrant clothing got his attention, so he watched the cart go by.

Sven noticed something in the stack of hay the cart was carrying. There was a movement from within the haystack. He told his colleague of his suspicion and reversed the car to stop the cart. The cart driver obeyed and stopped on the side of the road. He jumped off from his driving seat, patted his healthy-looking donkey, and treated it with a piece of carrot.

The officers explained quietly, in miming and pint-size English, about the "movement" inside his cart. With question lines appearing on his forehead, he led the officers to the back of the haul. From the side of the cart he took a rod and prodded into the hay. Behold, a man sat up, squinting his eyes due to the sudden daylight and with strands of hay in his hair. The cart driver was amazed and angry and stood there with wide-open, rolled eyes.

When the cart owner recovered from the shock, he shouted at the stowaway that it was not a wonder that his cart was going slowly. The officers intervened. Sven calmed the cart driver down. His colleague examined the stowaway to see that he was not carrying a weapon.

It was later found that he was a fare-dodger going to Famagusta port to be a fisherman. He described "fish" with wave movement with his hand, curved. He was not dangerous and was, in fact, a likeable man.

However, the cart driver pulled the man down from his cart and led him to the front, and he did something unusual—handed him the reins to drive the cart, while he rested with his tipple and enjoyed the sunshine. Duty reversed.

Sven and his workmate saw the cart drive off. They marvelled at it, shook their heads in wonder, and chortled. But easygoing life was not to continue. After some weeks, they were on alert for a demonstration.

The reporters were gathering in the vicinity of the Green Line divide around Famagusta Gate, which was selected for demonstration. The reporters had come from Cyprus and abroad, especially from countries representing the United Nations forces in Cyprus. The crowd on the Greek speaking side was gaining momentum.

The Turkish soldiers were on standby too on their side, with only no-man's-land separating them. They stood staunchly with upright shoulders and rifles in their hands. They stood there like statues. Even a pin stuck into their sides would not have made them twitch, but nonetheless, they were ready to spring into action and shoot if the demonstrators made a wrong move.

The peacekeeping officers with guns and batons created a line to act as a buffer between the Turks and the Greeks. They were here to control the crowd and stop anyone from crossing the buffer zone. It was tense. Sven was nervous. He did not want to see the crowd go out of control and run across the no-man's-land into Turkish-occupied territory. The opposite side would certainly shoot them. The Turkish soldiers relayed the message too by shooting into the air several times.

However, the Greek speaking side just wanted to make noises for international coverage. They were not armed with weapons; their missiles consisted of loud voices, megaphones, air horn trumpets, and cling-clang metallic utensils. They had a message for the Turkish occupied side.

They were chanting slogans and holding up placards that they wanted their land and properties back, that they desired a unified Cyprus, and that the Turkish occupation needed to end.

One man wore a bowler party hat with rainbow colours to represent all races and religions of Cyprus. He was a tall, muscular man and wore a shirt with the flag of Cyprus, which was a map of the island Cyprus and two olive branches representing peace. He had a mischievous look on his face, and to complement his patriotic hat, he wore rainbow-coloured, knee-length socks under his plain white Bermuda shorts, the white colour to represent peace again. Sarcastic and humorous placards were popping up from among the protesting crowd. Some of them read:

- "Where is my coffee jug? My coffee is not the same."
- "I have the key, you have the safe. Let's spend it."
- "I want my home and my neighbour back."
- "I left some goats behind and I have a gift for the grandkids."

And the rainbow-hat man held one above all heads that read:

- "Let's resolve this in Soho Town…"

(Soho Town is a red-light district in London, United Kingdom.)

And this protestor had a grin from ear to ear, and pointed out his billboard to a British reporter. The reporter instantly thought, *I could use it too as a pin-up in my office.* He wondered if they would even be able to concentrate in Soho Town, and he beamed at it.

The funny posters also brought a smile to Sven's face and the peacekeeping officers on duty. All seemed to be going well without a problem, and they did not have any serious issue to deal with. The demonstration went on peacefully throughout the afternoon. It slowly began to disperse, and finally, they all left as the sun went down. Alexis heard of it on the evening television news and saw Sven on the telly. Her heart fluttered, and she wanted to phone him but decided to wait.

Chapter 15

Sven and Alexis Maturing Together

Travelling together had made both Alexis and Sven more ripened and connected with each other and the outside world around them.

Sven and Alexis saw each other twice a month when Sven had a long break, but they talked regularly by phone if the coin box at Sven's base was free to use. The relationship was cementing. He was in love with her. He admired her for some of her attributes. She was a gutsy go-getter, faithful, and amicable, and additionally, she was fun to be with.

He related the nonconfidential incidents to her like a live commentator. The tales of his army life gave Alexis a further insight into his military life. He did not talk much about his work life due to his status, and Alexis did not press for it either. She understood the political climate and its sensitivity; plus, she was a party to it, even if she did not see it that way.

Alexis was back to her normal domestic jobs. Mrs. Williams was delighted to receive the decorative butterfly plate and hung it in the utility room. Andreas had bought one too for his grocery cart, but when he could not find a secure hanging space for it, he bestowed it on Grandma Cordelia. Alexis's landlord felt honoured in receiving a gift from his tenant; he intended to break the seal of the dessert wine bottle of muscat when he united with his business friends to sugarcoat them and, under intoxication, make himself believe that he was the King of Commerce—until someone decided to use laxatives on him again! Michael from Olynasa Pub appreciated his gift of a similar wine bottle too, which he said that he and Marsha would enjoy together. Alexis received a reflective idea; she had now thought of going into business with Andreas but had not mentioned this to him yet.

When she had to walk with her bicycle, either because of traffic or an uphill struggle, she would use this time constructively to reflect on her thoughts. She began to think of a name for her cleaning business. She chuckled at what she came up with—Pinafore Gritters! Yes, she would drive a small orange car with flashing amber lights with the name on it because the colour orange was associated with maintenance.

A car braked and hooted violently. Her mind had strayed off, and she had swayed into the middle of the road. The driver muttered at her in anger, flinging his right arm in the air and swirling it in motion, repeatedly tapping his head, a miming gesture to ask where her head was. It shook her up. She came back from her wandering realm and quickly moved back onto the side of the road; she certainly did not want to be gritted!

Sven Breaks Vital News

Then came the bombshell. Sven's assignment was coming to an end in Cyprus. He was to be transferred to be part of the United Nations peace-keeping force at the Iran-Iraq border, where the war had ended; the year was 1988. He would leave by the end of May the following year, if he decided to continue with the army. Christmas was around the corner, and Alexis wanted to go to England for Christmas, as she wished to be with her family, but Sven had planned to spend Christmas with her in Cyprus. Alexis was in turmoil regarding whom to please. Most of her employers were going for holiday too, so in the end, she opted for England to see her family for three weeks. Sven did not think Alexis would return but was thrilled when she phoned to tell him when she was coming back.

On her return to Larnaca airport, Sven was waiting with a bunch of flowers. He took her in a taxi to Nicosia and left her, as he was in a rush to get back to his base for his duties. He told her that he would be back in a few days' time, and he kept to his word. He came. The visit was to change his perception of a military life.

The following day on Saturday, Sven was on the front balcony of Alexis's bedsit, bent over the railings. He noted that there were a lot of different activities going on around him. On his left side was a United Nations contingency barracks, on the right side were young students playing cards, opposite was a grown-up couple arguing, and below came a loud voice talking on the telephone, as if the communication line was not clear and the phone call was to another country. Suddenly, he realised that this was the real world of people, instead of being on his own with a weapon in his hand, always on the alert for danger. He, at this point, had a deep realisation of the sparkle of life he was missing. Sven wanted to settle down and have a family of his own. He would leave the armed forces and go back to living a civilian life. He had now made up his mind about leaving the army, but he kept this to himself.

On Saturday evening, they walked to Olynasa Pub and had a good meal of lamb chops and chips with red wine. After they satisfied their hunger, Sven divulged to Alexis that he was not going to continue with military life and intended to return to Sweden as a civilian. There was a pause, and all they could hear was the music and the rattling noise of the cutlery in the background. Then Sven took both of Alexis's hands in his and asked her in a soft tone if she would like to come with him and live in Sweden. She was taken aback by his proposition, and she asked for time to mull over it—she didn't want to be influenced by the wine. She had to consider her future career. What would she do in Sweden without knowing how to speak Swedish? What work would she do? They talked about it, and Alexis asked him lots of questions, as she needed information to help her make up her mind.

Sven assured her that she would be able to start a business and suggested floristry and to enrol for a course on it. To put her doubts to rest, he told her that English was widely spoken in Sweden.

"Swedes love nature and flowers, and you will have a chance to experience Swedish culture too." He continued to educate her so as to instil enthusiasm in her. "The twinflower, or *Linnea borealis,* is the national flower of Sweden. The flowers are pink, bell-like, very fragrant, and grow in pairs—as we would if you gave us a chance to flourish together." Sven stroked her hands to reassure her that all would be well.

Alexis's head was whirring around nervously with this unexpected invitation. She pulled her hands away to prop herself up. She did not want to abandon Sven, but at the same time, the notion of moving to an unknown land was a big concern to her. She went silent in her thoughts while toying with the wineglass. If it did not work out, she could come back to Cyprus, but where would she live? She would have to bother her relatives again, which she was reluctant to do. She decided not to delve into the negativity. She informed Sven that she would give him a reply the next time they met, which was in two weeks' time. They toasted to the subsequent meeting, and Sven hoped eagerly to receive a fruitful reply.

To make up her mind, she visited the library to get information on Sweden. She also talked to Michael, who declined to give any advice due to the lesson he had previously learned regarding the ex-employer, the Francos. Finally, she was able to confide in Mrs. Ekstrom about her relationship with Sven, who was one of her countrymen. Mrs. Ekstrom was excited to hear of it and asked for his name to see if she knew him, but she didn't. She gave a pretty good picture of what to expect of Sweden culturally. Mrs. Ekstrom also conveyed to her that she should not be obligated to her job and to go if she wished to. Alexis was now closer to making up her mind than before.

Two weeks came, and Sven had to cancel his visit due to a cold spell of snow on the Troodos Mountains and rain and hail on the lowlands. January and February were the coldest months in Cyprus. When it snowed on the Troodos Mountains, it was the start of winter in Cyprus. According to the television news, this winter had a harsh twist to it.

Troodos was the largest mountain range in Cyprus, situated in the middle of the island at the dividing line with northern Cyprus; Mount Olympus was the highest peak. On mountain summits stood the Byzantine churches and monasteries, richly decorated with murals. It had charming villages with cobbled streets situated among vineyards and orchards of almond, apple, and cherry trees, which huddled in the valleys together with chalets hanging on terraced hill slopes covered with pine trees. An occasional wild sheep could be seen roaming in the hills. Soldiers on the Greek speaking side guarded their side of the Green Line nearby, which ran at the edge of the Troodos Mountains. A slice of nature would make an idyllic postcard picture, especially when it was covered in snow.

Broken Finger

Sven finally made his visit on the weekend. Alexis was excited to see him, and after a long hug and kiss, they headed for Olynasa Pub. It was early Saturday evening in January, and it was wintery, cold, and rainy. The pub was busy, and finding a private table was difficult. The floor space for dancing was tight too; dancing feet were on the go, and the usual Latin American music was playing, alternating with pop music. They found an empty table near a window.

Michael saw Sven and Alexis, and as soon as he became free from serving food, he approached them. He came and shook their hands. His hands were firm; they had hardened from the catering he did. Alexis jokingly pulled her hand away from his firm but enthusiastic handshake. Her hand rocketed towards the steel window frame and hit it with a landing force.

"Ouch!" she wailed as she felt the pain from the thump against the steel bar. It had hit her ring finger on her left hand, and it began to swell up. There was no pain at first, as it had become numb.

Sven came to her aid, and Michael hurriedly got ice cubes and cloth. Later, he returned with a roll of soft surgical cloth tape, scissors, and a safety pin. Michael left this to Sven, as he had to attend to the guests. He was apologetic about his departure, and Alexis insisted that he attend to his business, as she would be fine with her soldier companion. It was an opportunity to see how caring and considerate Sven was. Could Sven do better with a hand bandage than the man carrying a king-size mattress for his mother-in-law? He was going to be tested on his nurturing experience.

Sven used his army training skills and dabbed her finger and the surrounding arm with a cloth ice wrap. Ice would reduce swelling and lessen the pain by numbing the area around it. He wrapped the bandage tightly around her four fingers together to stop the displacement of the fractured bone. He proceeded to place it in a sling around her neck. When completed, she sat with only one hand in use now. Thankfully, it was her nondominant left hand that was injured. Both now needed cheering up and to relax, after Sven's trial of nursing care. He was successful in Alexis's eyes. However, her mood changed swiftly too, like the crashing waves of tsunami. It was not the best time of the month for her either.

Alexis soon realised that she only had one hand to use, and she became irritable and began to take it out on Sven, complaining annoyingly about Michael, who was busy in his kitchen. Sven purchased Carlsberg, and Bellapais for Alexis, as he knew she liked it. But she shoved the glass back to him, asked him to drink it himself, and sat there with a long, sullen face with eyes ablaze. Sven left her alone and drank his beer in silence, waiting for the sulk to melt. Her hand had become numb from the pain, but the sensitivity of the soreness was building up slowly. Alexis eventually took her glass back and sipped her Bellapais. It tasted delightful to her dry, angry throat, and gradually the sulk evaporated and gaiety condensed. Michael peered to see what was up. He had escaped Alexis's wrath.

However, the following day the broken ring finger became very painful. It had swollen up. Sven called a taxi and took her to the hospital emergency room. An orthopaedics doctor saw her, and X-rays showed the finger had a bone fracture and part of the hand was affected too. Her left hand, excluding the thumb, was placed in a cast extending to the elbow, then placed in a sling hanging from her neck. This ensured the bone remained fixed in place, so the broken bone would heal straight, back to its original state. She was also given painkillers and asked to come back after two weeks. Sven had to leave, and he did not receive his answer to his invitation to Sweden. She was in no mood to answer him, and he did not delve into it either.

Alexis could not use her bicycle now and had to travel by bus. Some of her workplaces were in the suburbs and out of reach of the bus stops, so she had to walk quite a distance to get to her work. Fortunately, it was her left hand, so it did not completely hinder her work, but it slowed her down. She stayed longer than her usual time, which she didn't mind. Her employers were sympathetic towards her and gave her a hand wherever they could. When she needed her two hands at work, she used the elbow of her bandaged hand. It made her reflect on the plight of disabled people.

After two weeks, the second set of X-rays was taken with the cast on, and the previous hand mould and sling had to remain in place for four more weeks. She was advised not to use her broken finger, as the fractured bone needed to reset, and to return after a month. She began to use her bicycle, though, with one hand, which was dangerous. But she did more walking than cycling, as she could not use the brakes.

The weeks in a cast and sling were unbearable. Alexis only used the bicycle on level roads and when the roads were not busy. If she had to make an emergency stop, she used her feet to stop the bicycle, so she had to ride at a slow pace. This meant too that she had to wear shoes with thick rubber soles. She at times had to walk with her bicycle up a hill using the side pavement. When she got exhausted, she looked backwards and could see the town of Nicosia spread out below her, which encouraged her to continue, as it gave her satisfaction on her achievement.

After some days, Alexis was in the car queue on a flat road and riding slowly with her one hand. At a T-junction, the car ahead of her made a sudden stop, and her emergency foot stop was not able to halt the bicycle, so she ended up colliding with the car ahead of her, which was a junker ready for the scrapyard. Alexis's head bumped into the battered car's back bonnet. Behind her was a posh car, and its female driver began to hoot, as if that was going to stop the accident when it had already happened. Or was it a warning to her expensive head not to run into the bicycle? The driver of the junk car, a college student, came out angrily to view if there was any damage to his patchy old car. He was more concerned about an extra dent to his car than Alexis's well-being.

How foolish he was! His car was already beaten up. An extra knock would not bring the scrap price down, and questionable too if metal recyclers would pay much in the first place for this car.

Fortunately, it was a light collision and caused no added destruction to his treasured car. Alexis braced herself and quickly walked off with her bicycle from the side of the road. Her hand hurt. She sought to look as normal as possible, as she did not want the police to get involved. She managed to walk away from the incident with a slight bruise to her forehead and an aching hand, but she was shaken up. The arm cast had mercifully shielded the injured hand.

Finally, the day came when the cast came off. At last she could use her fingers again for the stiff handbrakes, and once more she could cook a proper meal too. Sven suggested that she go to a steam or dry heat sauna for therapeutic benefits, as saunas eased joint pains and stiffness, reduced stress and fatigue, and had other health gains. She searched for information on a sauna in the area and found one. It was none other than the Body Bella, which she was already aware of. This was the same beauty parlour that had conveniently misspelt the name and called it Body Sensual to get attention. It certainly got Alexis's attention now, and she giggled at the thought of how it had worked out for them.

One free Monday afternoon, Alexis set out for one of one of the branches of Body Bella, pushing her bicycle on the pavement, as it looked risky to ride on the road and she still had to practice using her other hand. It was midafternoon, and for some older ones, it was resting time even in the Mediterranean mild winter, but not for a man in his early sixties who was riding a three-wheeled scooter on the pavement. She had just passed him by going off onto the quiet main road and joining the raised pavement again to avoid bumping into him. All of a sudden, she heard laughter, and she turned around to see him waving his hand and pointing towards her clothing. Alexis stopped. She thought her skirt had become loose at the back and he was having a cheeky peep at it. No, it was not that. She glanced around her skirt, and on the left side she saw a large product label with the clip still on. It was for a denture glue fixer!

The tag with the metallic clip had become magnetised to the clothing and was attached to the woollen skirt. Alexis had picked it up from the chemist, which she had visited to buy more painkillers. The denture glue was advertised in large print to make the product sell fast and so weak eyes could spot it!

It made Alexis look odd and a comic sight on the street where people did not behave in a silly manner. People were conservative here on the island.

Alexis joined in with the laughter as the older man on the scooter caught up with her. "I thought you were advertising a new brand," he chortled. "I will be needing this soon."

This made Alexis laugh more and confirmed that she wasn't upset. She stopped and embarrassedly removed the label from her skirt and placed it in the basket at the front. He talked to her for a while, asking her where she was going. She told him briefly of her destination, and in a gruff tone, he went, "Aaaahh, you mean Body Sensual. I know that one. It was in the newspaper."

Alexis quickly corrected him of the name—it was Body Bella—and informed him of the shop's health purpose. And neither did she waste time in publicising her work, as her job schedule was unpredictable. Mrs. Williams's visitors had departed, and her work was reduced again, and people like this scooter man, whose name was Costas Stavros, could be effective in spreading the news for her. He was in great excitement and nearing his retirement age. He requested her telephone number, expressing to her that he might need her one day.

No, he won't, contemplated Alexis with amusement. *He will phone me but more to natter and for a laugh.* She gave him the phone number, though.

He also told her that he could walk and dance, but since his journey today was a distance away and as he was feeling lazy, he was using his scooter to go to a cafeteria for a Greek coffee.

Was he hinting for company?

She joked with a touch of lighthearted sarcasm, "You sure will need an extra strong, sweet coffee, Varee Glykos, to boost your energy level."

He chuckled, hooted at that statement, and started to leave. The happy man pushed on his accelerator pedal, and Alexis left for her own speedy therapeutic boost in a sauna. He sped off to have Greek coffee, which is served in a demitasse cup and saucer with a glass of water.

Alexis had not forgotten her food voucher for the potato chips from the kebab shop. After her sauna, she decided to use her credit note to get her food exchange.

She went to the cafeteria, and the door opened with ease. It had been fixed. Demetriou, the counter staff, was with a young husky man, and on seeing her, he quickly signalled with facial gestures to warn Alexis of the man stationed next to him. He was his boss. Alexis got the hint and ordered tea instead of handing over her food voucher. She waited for the boss to leave and approached Demetriou. He exchanged the credit note in a business-like manner and gladly offered her fried chips; he showed no jovialness this time, as he was tired. Alexis had her bag of cooked chips and left quietly.

Odena Hotel

The working weeks fell into a routine. Nothing out of the norm took place. There was no phone call either from Costas, the scooter man, as anticipated. But there was an addition to the job. Michael referred her to a hotel job at Odena Hotel. She had her Mondays off, but she let it go for this hotel role. Instead, she had Tuesdays off, as Mrs. Williams had gone quiet with work. The Williams family was having a problem with the landlord, who was in the process of raising the rent. So far, Alexis was thankful that her landlord was not being greedy.

Monday came, and she went to work at the Odena Hotel, which was in the old part of the city and could not be missed, as it was painted pink.

She was given a uniform to wear and an assignment for Room M on the third floor. It was for the manager, right at the top, and consisted of a small penthouse. She had her cleaning items and knocked at the door. There was no answer, so she proceeded with her master key. She opened the door, and inside she was startled to see a middle-aged man with a halo of flowers, cream and gold, on his head, doing a jig in a circle.

"Kalimera." He welcomed her in Greek.

"Kalimera," she replied bashfully.

He was still in his pyjamas, waltzing on his own to instrumental Greek music playing in the background. To Alexis, it looked like he had a Christmas wreath on his head. Christmas had gone, though. As she stood there bemused, he stretched out his hand to her, motioning her to join him in the dance. This eccentric gentleman was Costas Stavros, the scooter man, and he was the proprietor of the hotel!

Alexis giggled, took her multicoloured duster, and danced with it in one hand and joined the eccentric gentleman with the other hand—what a colourful sight, a wreath and duster! She danced for a while but then had to leave him, as she had work to do in this three-bedroom penthouse. She dashed off to perform her duties. Costas had said that he could dance, and he could. His wife was out of town visiting her family and would be for some weeks. She probably needed a rest from him. Once inside the quaint bedroom, partially filled with mirrored wardrobes, she checked whether the mattress had gone with her too, like the mother-in-law she had come across on one of her hitchhiking sprees! A mattress was present, though, or was it replaced? Alexis pondered with amusement.

A maid knocked to deliver a letter with no name on it—only the address. Costas took it in his hand and yelped. Alexis came to a standstill. He sounded as if he had been electrocuted! Alexis went to investigate the commotion. He had recognised the familiar handwriting; it was from his wife.

"I wrote down the address for her and left my name out," he said in a high-pitched voice and laughed. "I thought she would remember my name and place it herself on the envelope, but of course she didn't." Alexis giggled. His wife had written an endearing letter instead of phoning him.

She went back to the master bedroom and saw on the dressing table a portrait photograph in black and white of both of them. His young wife had been an attractive and elegant lady, with short hair curved at the neckline; her earrings and necklace were probably made of pearls. Next to her was Costas, a young man in a suit. From the bedroom, Alexis asked him his wife's name.

"Maria," he replied with great pride.

Alexis reflected on their relationship and concluded, "Distance does make a heart grow fonder."

He showed her other photographs on the wall. He was now feeling tired, so he used a wooden walking stick with a crook handle. One was of their wedding day, and some photos were with their three children. The place was like a museum of their years together. It seemed they had had happy years. The room was cluttered with pinewood shelves, potted plants, and carpets. The potted plants consisted of the island's purple orchids, and the Cyprus green plant sat gracefully in a pebbled clay container. Carpets were rolled up during hot days and put away in the storage room and brought out again when the weather became cold, as it was now. The kitchen had black-chequered marble floor tiles and worktops. The kitchen had its own balcony for a gulp of fresh air when cooking. It had kitchen cupboards with carved engravings, cream in colour. The large lounge decorated with ivory-coloured sofas had an outlet to a second balcony. This had outdoor wicker sofas with red cushions, but its view from the balcony was blocked by the taller building next door.

Alexis had a huge job on her hand to get the penthouse looking good and smelling fresh for his wife. She was returning soon, and he was delighted at this, displaying the excitement through his hops with the walking stick and lifting the stick in the air every now and again as he danced to the music. Alexis had to get going with her work, as she was accountable to a house supervisor downstairs, who came upstairs at intervals to check on her progress. Mr. Stavros's eccentricity was well known, so his behaviour was nothing unusual for the long-term staff. They respected and liked him.

Downstairs was a different world of constant smiles and saying hello to passing visitors. In the kitchen, they had to bear with the cluttering noise of kitchen utensils and staff talking loudly across the lengthy kitchen when not busy. If something went wrong, out came a flurry of corrupt words, which only made people laugh.

Alexis finished the penthouse in the afternoon, and by now, Costas had dressed up and was downstairs in his office, keeping a tab on the income and expenses for the day. Alexis was given one more room downstairs to make spick-and-span, and she would not be back until the following week. To get the rooms ready after the weekend was a once-a-week job. The hotel was also occupied by the blue beret soldiers who came to the city for fun and company.

When she finished, she had her meal. It was a plateful of salad and *mousakka*, made of layers of aubergine and minced meat. She got changed, received her payment, and off she went on her bicycle. Sven's visit was due soon, and Alexis looked forward to it, but she still had to let him know whether she was going to accompany him to Sweden or not.

Alexis's Response to the Proposition

It was February now. Sven came with a group of friends, and they all stayed at Odena Hotel. They had come to celebrate a birthday party of a girlfriend of one of the soldiers who worked at the hotel. Sven phoned Alexis on Friday evening from a coin box to announce that he had arrived. He was waiting to receive an answer from Alexis about his proposition. Alexis had that reply now.

When he phoned, Alexis invited him for an evening meal at seven the following day and asked him to come hungry.

Sven came in his civilian clothes. He was on time, keeping up with his Swedish tradition of not being late when invited. He took a gift, in this case a box of Belgian chocolates. As he came up the stairs of Alexis's building, he passed a bulky man on the way, and he looked at him questioningly. Back in the bedsit, after the greetings with kisses, he quizzed her as to who he was. She told him amusingly that he was her landlord, who had come to collect the rent and to banter, probably a day's laugh for him, since he was working in a hectic environment. Sven beamed, and they sat down inside a warm, neat place, heated with mobile gas heaters, and he noted that the butterfly plate from Rhodes Island was hanging on the wall.

Alexis presented him with a delightful meal as a gesture for his friendship. She had Cypriot wines, cabernet sauvignon, and shiraz to start him with, followed by quite a special meal: *bourgouri* soup, made from wheat grains and spices, fried fish served with winter vegetables of potatoes, mushrooms, and spinach, with a salad plate of black-eyed beans, lettuce, tomatoes, and feta cheese. The meal ended with *loukoumades,* a Cypriot sweet dish, similar to a doughnut with honey, and, of course, coffee for Swedish Sven and tea for British Alexis! Now he desired his sweet answer to his previous offer.

When the atmosphere had calmed down and the used crockery, plain yellow in colour, and coffee-brown lap trays were out of the way, he calmly brought up the subject and asked her if she had decided whether to join him in Sweden. Then came the most nerve-wracking reply he had been waiting for. Alexis made her pronouncement.

"Yes, I will come with you to Sweden."

Sven was exuberant and toasted to joy and a new beginning, subtly represented by the yellow-coloured crockery. He took her outside to the balcony, kissed her, and held her up in the air. The couple from the opposite balcony, a chubby, medium-height lady dressed in maroon and a thin, tall man with a pulled-out white shirt and black baggy trousers, came outside hurriedly to see what the commotion was.

"You should do what that man is doing to her," she whined, pointing towards Sven and Alexis's twirl in the air.

Her towering husband twitched his moustache, lifted his eyebrows, bent down to look straight in his wife's eyes, and laughingly told her, "*Agape mou* [My darling], I would become like a flat pitta bread!" He greatly emphasized the word flat. They both chortled and went in. They gave a deep sigh of relief that it was not the Turkish soldiers from across the Green Line invading them.

Chapter 16

Troodos Mountains

The Troodos Mountains were ideal for snow lovers. These snow enthusiasts came in various forms: skiiers, snow hikers, tobogganers, children playing in snow, and grandparents sitting in cafeterias sipping wine or drinking Greek or machine-brewed coffee, appreciating the fresh air or taking great delight in the snow-covered picturesque villages. In winter, Troodos was dreamlike with its mountainous scenery, terraced villages, and welcoming air of quietness and tranquillity.

Throughout the year, it bustled with daily life, catering to the visitors with souvenir shops, food, accommodation, and wine export. When the snow melted in early spring at the end of March, the fruit trees blossomed, wild flowers covered the mountainsides, the waterfalls made a rushing sound, birds created a rhythmic hum, and lonesome goats wandered, announcing their presence with tinkling bells. Spring provided a green environment and fresh mountain air filled with a fragrant scent from the black pine and juniper trees.

Sven arranged a weekend away with Alexis to the mountain ranges for the end of February. He booked a hotel near Troodos Square. This now meant Alexis had to buy clothing and boots for the snow. At the same time, she was being prepared for a life in Sweden. Alexis took Saturday off, and they travelled by bus from Nicosia to the Troodos Mountains, which took around ninety minutes, allowing for the stops on the way. Snuggled in warm clothing, they settled down to watch the agricultural landscape pass by. One local elderly passenger kindly offered them an insulated container of coffee, which they politely declined.

Once in Troodos, they checked into their hotel and changed into snow clothing. They managed to get a lift on a tourist coach to the Sun Valley car park for the ski hut. They travelled this way instead of using the walking trail, which would have taken them around twenty minutes.

The ski hut was on the beginner's slope under Mount Olympus. It had a cafeteria, and next to it was a ski shop owned by the Cyprus ski club. They had reasonable time for skiing before the ski lifts closed at 4:00 p.m., so they proceeded to the ski shop to buy a daily ski pass and hire skis for Sven and a snow sledge for Alexis, since she was a novice at snow sports.

There was enough powdery snow on the mountains for snow activities. The previous night had seen fifty centimetres of snow. They made their way from the ski hut via a ski lift to reach the top of the Aphrodite slopes, suitable for beginners at skiing but also used for sledges. Sven first gave Alexis a hand in tobogganing down the slope, and they had a good laugh at it, as they fell off a couple of times—once toppled by Sven on purpose. Then, with great amusement, he spotted a Greek priest! He was a tall man with a long grey beard and a long blue cassock over layers of warm clothing. He wore a chimney pot hat. He was not wearing a crucifix; the pectoral cross was given to specific priests for faithful services. He had a welcoming smile and was entertaining children with a snowman and snowballs.

Sven went up to him and asked if he could take care of Alexis while he went skiing. He told him that Alexis was a novice with skiing. The priest, who spoke reasonable English, agreed and made a traditional sign of a cross on his chest. He had asked for help from above, which brought a smile to both of them. Sven told Alexis that he would meet her at a cafeteria and pointed below towards it. He, now feeling at ease about Alexis, skied a short distance away to another ski lift to transport him and his skis to the top of the Hermes slope; the hill was meant for skiers at an intermediate level. Awaiting Sven was an elating sensation from gliding smoothly down the piste with the gust of wind blowing against his goggled face, as the glowing sunlight filtered through the winter sky, encasing the snow-covered mountaintops and pine trees on the horizon, staging an enthralling view. It was a thrilling escape from normal army life.

Alexis had her own thrills too. The priest jumped in the large toboggan (called a sledge) with Alexis cheerfully at the back, hiding behind the chimney pot hat, and off they went for a taste of an adrenaline buzz for Alexis. They both went sliding down, with children running after them, throwing snowballs, especially at the priest. Alexis shouted and screamed from the fun she was having, and then both would walk up again, Alexis pulling the sledge behind her. After some rides, the priest decided to rest and left her to play with the children, but he came back to borrow her toboggan to take the children down the track. Everyone was having glorious fun.

Nature Trails

The priest eventually began to look tired, and Alexis invited him for refreshment at the cafeteria, the meeting place previously arranged by Sven. It had a warm, tranquil feel to it, with refreshing scenery of snow-covered pine trees and frosty mountain slopes in the distance. They both ordered *gluvine,* a hot, mulled red wine, popular in German-speaking countries and France. In Scandinavia, it was known as *glögg.* This drink was warming and good at beating the winter chill. It would soon be dark, as days were shorter, which meant longer times in pubs and coffee shops.

The priest got into a conversation with her about the holidays, and they talked about the four main nature trails from the Troodos Mountains for nature lovers and hikers, as he was.

"Some of the trails lead through little streams and waterfalls. The fresh mountain air and the fragrance of cedars, pines, and cypress forests are an exceptional experience," he commented.

He stopped to take a gulp of air flowing in through the entrance door opening and closing. He had a sip of mulled wine and continued talking. "Other trails lead through fauna and flora and fields, leading to tiny painted Byzantine churches on the Troodos Mountains. Most of them are under the protection of UNESCO. Kykkos is the most famous and wealthiest of the monasteries in Cyprus, and it is well worth a visit."

Alexis asked about him. He said that he was from one of Troodos's old monasteries, in Omodos. With enthusiasm, he said, "Monasteries were purposely built in the mountains, away from the vulnerable coastline."

A white cat ambled by to sit close to the priest's feet, and he looked down to stroke the cat. Since cats had good night vision and sense of smell, it was very likely the cat had marked the priest's presence, as he must have been a regular and welcomed visitor to the cafeteria to get the blessing.

Sven strode briskly into the cafeteria with his skiis and poles. He turned back hurriedly, taking with him Alexis's sledge. It was getting dark, and he had to return them to the ski hire shop. On the way out, he asked Alexis to order him what she and the priest were drinking, as it smelled good. Alexis ordered the spiced red wine for Sven and baklava, a diamond-shaped, sweet pastry filled with nuts and honey, for the three of them. Alexis wanted to hear more from the priest, so she knew she had to find a way to keep him talking, and that was through food. The priest did not ask for their names and neither did Sven and Alexis probe into his; he likely met a lot of people every day, and he would need rolls of memory tape if he had to remember their names.

Sven returned, dusting the snowflakes from his coat, and settled down to have his mulled wine. He joined the conversation with the priest. The cleric stuck to his holiday theme and told them of the carnival time in March, which celebrated grape harvest, wine making, nature, and beauty.

The priest paused to inquire of their social backgrounds and found out that they were leaving for Sweden after March, so he continued to give them a taste of Cyprus spring. He informed Sven and Alexis of the ten days of carnival time in Limassol.

"It is a festive season with joyful celebration, decorative floats, lively street procession, and fancy dress costumes and balls."

Alexis giggled and added, "I am sure Andreas, the grocery man, would love to go to this procession in a fancy costume, and if he could, he would take his decorative cart too."

She went on to tell the priest about Andreas, and some of it was new knowledge for Sven. They laughed.

The priest continued, "There is a massive dummy King Carnival at the Limassol carnival who welcomes visitors, and he returns on the last day to bid farewell."

Alexis joined in, excited. "This is definitely Andreas's forte, and perhaps I should rent out a fancy dress costume and venture with him to carnival town and join the procession, as I am sure he will be going."

Sven chortled and teased her to take photographs to show him. Sven felt uneasy about it, though. The priest sensed Sven's change of mood and that it was time to leave, as it had gone dark outside. He bid them farewell with a blessing for a safe journey back. The couple had to depart too and opted for a meal at a tavern in Troodos Village in front of a furnace fire before getting a lift to take them back.

In the relaxing warmth of the fire cuddled next to Sven, Alexis lit up suddenly, as she had a funny idea of how to dress up for the Limassol carnival procession. She would dress up as an impish nun! Sven laughed.

Travelling around Troodos

The subsequent day was frosty and snowy, but the early morning sun beaming through the pine and juniper trees left a glowing star hanging over some of the snow-covered trees, and the sunrays broke through the gaps in the branches. What a glorious sight it was up in the mountains. Sven and Alexis stood there for a while admiring the beauty of it until a jeep hooted to announce its arrival.

Sven decided to spend his day skiing, whereas Alexis chose a private jeep tour. She had heard of this four-wheeled excursion from the hotel receptionist, who had contacted the driver on her behalf. There was place for one, and Alexis accepted it quickly and paid the receptionist. Peter, the driver, was an ex-British army officer living in the Troodos. He knew the area well. Alexis took her seat at the back of the cleaned-up army jeep.

In the jeep was also an English couple with a cute, blond preschool-age child holding on to a toy train. The husband sat in the front seat with Peter, and his wife with the child occupied the back-seat with Alexis. All that was exchanged from the passengers was a polite hello to Alexis as she boarded the jeep. She sat in the backseat with the child in the middle and the mother on the side behind the driver. Sven and Alexis arranged to meet at the hotel restaurant and parted with a kiss. The passengers did not seem to be in a mood to converse with strangers and neither was Alexis. The car radio was on, broadcast from the British base, which was familiar to them. Alexis remembered what a contrasting welcome she had had when she hitchhiked from Faliraki on Rhodes Island in a truck.

The trip was to take them to a town and nearby mountain villages. Some of the villages were unspoilt by tourism, but some had conformed to commercialism.

Paphos and Omodos

The group's first stop was at Paphos. It was a long drive from Troodos of around an hour to this seaside town. Here, they experienced an untouched, wonderful view of the port with the medieval castle in the background and visited the amphitheatre. UNESCO had added the whole town to its list of World Heritage sites.

They then headed towards the charming village of Omodos. The two men sitting in the front had warmed up and began to converse with each other, letting out a cackle every now and again. The ladies at the back were consumed by the scenery and allowed their minds to drain away amid the adult noise. The child made childlike noises as he happily ran his toy train on the floorboard. The mother kept a watchful eye on the child for his safety and remained reserved and quiet. She mostly communicated with courteous smiles; Alexis's mouth had now become weary from returning the "Pan-Am air hostess" smile.

At Omodos, free wine samples welcomed them. Alexis thought that perhaps the wine might break through the icy atmosphere. Omodos was a wine-producing village with pretty-looking cobble paths and picturesque Mediterranean houses with old ladies sitting outside making lace. There was a monastery in the centre of the village. The wood-crafted verandas were filled in the summer with coloured flower pots, giving them a vibrant appearance. But above all, the town was known for its hospitality. The Greek priest they had met on the snow slopes was from this monastery. Alexis took this village to her heart as an ideal place to get married. She now began to think of marriage. This had not crossed her mind before.

They stopped for a meal at a tavern in the village and had a polite conversation. Back in the jeep, the tourist group gazed quietly, taking pictures of the scenery, and the child was well behaved, sometimes babbling to his imaginary train driver and rail users or sitting in his mum's lap chewing a lollipop. The jeep passengers did not say much on the whole and went along to wherever the British driver was taking them. He was absorbed in concentrating on the driving.

Platres and Kakopetria

They were now driving towards Platres on a levelled gravel road, and in the calmness of the passing landscape, they were taken by surprise by a loud blast. The steering wheel jerked, and the car began to weave at a faster speed. The experienced driver knew what had happened.

"A back tyre has blown out," the driver said as he concentrated hard on the steering wheel. With firmly gripped hands, he took control of it. He kept looking ahead at the horizontal road and pointed the car as straight as possible to keep it in a straight line. There was a silent panic on the faces of the passengers.

The husband said, "Do not slam on the brakes, as it will put the car into a spin and go out of control. Let the car roll to a stop itself."

The husband turned around swiftly to have a look at his wife and son. The wife was clutching the child in her lap. Her face was frozen and eyes filled with fear. Alexis gaped; her heart throbbed in fear. There was no screaming, as it would have confused the driver. The road was not wide and had a gradual drop on the left side where the car was, and there were no barriers to stop it from rolling over. It was a frightening situation. Thankfully, there was no oncoming car, and ice and snow had melted, as the road had been gritted with rock salt. Rock salt stopped ice forming and caused the ice or snow to melt. It is also more effective if vehicles and pedestrians flattened the surface, as was fortunately the case here.

The driver restrained the car well and was glad that he had been driving slowly when the tyre blew. The car gradually came to a stop, and there was a genuine, deep sigh of relief. The driver immediately placed the hazard lights on, and everyone disembarked. He took out two triangular breakdown signs and placed them in front of and behind the car. The child began to cry, and the mother calmed him down by getting him a lollipop from her carrier bag in the car. The lovely scenery around them with Platres in sight made up for the misadventure for the women, as they also watched the two men get down to repair the tyre.

The driver was well equipped for breakdowns. The two men jacked the car to change to another winter wheel, which gave a better grip in cold and wet weather. A small van transporting seasonal produce for the hotels in Platres passed by, and the two men stopped to give them help too. With eight helping hands, they were back on the road shortly. There was not much time left for daylight now, and it was getting cold too.

They drove to Platres. It was in the foothills of the Troodos Mountains, an old village, well-known for the visits of some famous people. It had pretty waterfalls, attractive buildings, and beautiful scenery. It was also acknowledged for its chocolate factory, and all visitors were given a free tasting tour of chocolate dips. They also stopped for a well-deserved break for a flavoured local drink and bite: *zivania* with *meze*, a platter of local dips eaten with a piece of pitta bread. Zivania went down well with the driver, as it is a warming-up drink during the cold months of winter, especially in the Troodos.

While enjoying their respite, they watched a short play on display. They were told that it was about a taxman and a clown. The burly and slightly bald taxman dragged a thin clown by his ear to pay taxes. The clown made miming hand actions, knocking towards the side of his head with his finger, to tell the audience that the taxman was talking nonsense. He tied the taxman with a rope and dragged him to the green cardboard tax office, and two puppets appeared at the window and hit the taxman with mini beanbags on his head. The message was that it was he, the taxman, who had to pay the taxes first! Everyone laughed, including the wife, and the child clapped his hands, giggling away and, at times, clinging to his mother's arm and burying his face into it. At last the wife laughed! They were all now on their way down "Icebreaker Avenue."

They learned from the driver about Platres's history and that during the British control of Cyprus, Platres was used as a hill resort to escape from the summer heat of the coast.

After saying good-bye to Platres, they headed northward to the village of Kakopetria, north of the Troodos Mountains. In winter, it provided a peaceful and tranquil atmosphere, with fireplaces in houses and hotels warming the place.

During hot coastal months, the cool mountainous climate and picturesque landscape with the red-tiled roofs of wooden-and-stone houses drew the attention of rich families to come for the summer and enjoy the freshness and beauty. At the village pub, they asked for the homemade wine called *caraff*. Snow began to fall, and the tour of the day had to come quickly to an end.

They took their seats in the jeep, which turned around to finally go back to Troodos Village. The jeep's road lights were on. The vehicle persevered through the snow-covered route and eventually reached the village. Alexis got off near Troodos Square and trailed in the snow to her hotel. The family was driven to their nearby resort too. The child was asleep by now. Alexis felt the trip had been totally worthwhile, as it had given her a general idea of the Troodos hilly villages, and now she had a story to tell Sven.

On the way to her hotel, Alexis met a well-rounded, middle-aged man who was drunk and staggering as he tried to reach his hotel room. Two male staff members helped get him to his room amid his raucous ranting and singing that he was "as big and old as the oldest juniper tree found in Cyprus, which is eight hundred years old!"

This man was part of the walking group that had gone snow hiking on the Atlante Nature Trail, which circled Mount Olympus starting from Troodos Square. From one vantage point, one can have a spectacular view of the entire island. After some hours, the trailers ended at a tavern. This "juniper tree" man now had had so much to drink that he needed help to get to his room.

It was dark already and snow was falling, and Sven had not arrived yet. He had stopped by for a drink with the trailers and ended up talking to a Scandinavian girl who was working there. It was rare for a local girl to work in a pub, so foreign girls were given visas to work. He got carried away with conversation and flirting, and forgot that Alexis could be back.

And, she was waiting, worried. The tables were turning around from the Faliraki experience, when the bus driver had left her behind. Thoughts were going round in her head. *What if he had a ski accident? No, maybe he got lost. Perhaps he is waiting for me at the square.* Then a gnawing feeling gripped her that it could be a girl. She decided to wait. And it was risky to go out in the snow.

Alas, he came. He arrived swaying in on the hands of the blond girl. Alexis at first thought that he was hurt, and worried lines appeared on her forehead. The girl handed Sven and his skis over to Alexis without a word. Alexis surged with jealousy. She was the same girl—the dazzling beauty Sven had left her to dance with in Ayia Napa when she had gone there with Molly.

When Sven came closer, his breath revealed that he had been drinking alcohol. She was more deeply disturbed. And he blabbered about only having a drink with the girl. An argument flared up between the two. He assured her that nothing had happened, but she did not believe him. The male hotel staff watched with amusement at the day's drunk sessions.

Alexis left him angrily and headed for the hotel restaurant to eat, and on the way asked the male staff to help Sven and carry his skis to the room. They agreed. The two men wondered if he too would sing as the previous one had, and he did! He sang the Swedish drinking song "Helan Går" while he staggered down his route. In the room, upon Sven's request, the men led him to the bathroom. They also advised him to drink lots of water to replace lost water and gave him a spoon of olive oil before he hit the pillow. Olive oil is a Mediterranean way of preventing hangovers; the fat in the olive oil limits the body's absorption of alcohol.

They were to leave Troodos the next day. The night was long, Sven was asleep, and Alexis occupied it with packing up their luggage. And she vented her anger by throwing his clothes into his baggage.

The following day, Monday morning, Sven was hungry, and he walked into the breakfast room after Alexis. He sat at a different table, as Alexis's table was full. She ignored him and did not go and join him. Sven was not in a mood for any further squabbles either. He had lots of water, and after gorging on a healthy breakfast with toast, he had picked himself up. But he still had to conquer another "gremlin": silence.

They departed for Nicosia by bus at nine in the morning, in silence. Sven tried to cheer Alexis and fondled her earlobe. She shrugged him off. Mountain goats were springing on the hillside parallel to the moving bus, and Sven sprang into action too. He pointed out the goats to Alexis to get attention, but she snubbed him. He then began conversing with the goats through the window.

"Hello, Snowflake. Do you want to come and sit next to me? You go '*baah baah baah*' and I go '*huh huh huh*.' We both create a harmonious melody." It seemed the effect of the drinking song was still on him. Alexis could not help giggling, and she gave in after a time of sulking and sang, "*Baah baah baah.*"

In harmonious blend, he added, "*Huh huh huh,*" and it caught on with other nearby bus passengers, who joined in, divided in two sections. And one who had a soprano voice belted it out.

Sven and Alexis at last made up with a kiss and both sang to each other, in the midst of the noise, in the melodious tune, "I love you, I love you, I l-o-v-e you," pointing an assuring finger at each other. The passengers continued for a while with the melody of imitating animal sounds (onomatopoeia), and gave up laughing.

As the return journey continued, both felt as refreshed and attentive as the goats' tinkling bells on the mountainsides. Alexis's endearing name was to be Snowflake.

Both got cuddly and began to discuss their thoughts. Travelling together had united their hearts and revived them deeply, and they discussed what they would do in Sweden. From travelling around, they now had the desire to advise others, and both agreed on a travel industry.

Alexis added, "I will learn the Swedish language and then do a travel course to give me an understanding of the travel business, and then gradually introduce my cleaning business, Pinafore Gritters."

"Yes, very good idea," responded Sven convincingly. He added, "With determination, we can do it."

Seeing the beautiful Mediterranean architecture on their travels had sharpened Sven's desire to have a home and to fill it with the pitter-patter of little feet. Sven wanted to probe to make sure that Alexis wasn't coming to Sweden for just another travel venture. He wanted to take a step further with her, so he initiated the prenuptial discussion. She was taken aback.

But, unknown to Sven, Alexis had a psychological fear to overcome.

Chapter 17

Carnival and Farewells to Her

Employers

Once in Nicosia, Alexis continued with her daily jobs, and with Sven's help, she began to plan her departure for Sweden. But Alexis had one more adventure, an idea given birth by the priest on Troodos Mountains. Sven could not get time off so soon, and he was not keen on joining her for the carnival in Limassol, which was at the beginning of March. So she took her idea to her friend Andreas. He had already made plans to go to the parade on Carnival Sunday on his own; he had split from Greta. Carnival was his speciality, so how could he miss it? Alexis agreed to join him for that Sunday procession.

Alexis knew what she wanted for her carnival costume and went to visit a fancy dress shop in Nicosia to rent it. Andreas was there in the shop too. Since they were not entering a competition, their costumes did not need a secret tag.

Andreas asked her, "What are you dressing up as?"

With a mischievous expression on her face, she answered with a chuckle, "As a naughty nun with a glittering mask." He chortled, and she continued in a funny tone, "Nobody will be able to recognise me. And you?"

"I am dressing up as what I am good at—that is, being an ice cream cone," replied Andreas impishly. "I will be that fresh guy for someone. I wonder if nuns have ice cream?" They both chuckled at this, but Alexis did not have an answer.

"What an odd combination! A nun and an ice cream cone!" Alexis marvelled. She wondered how long the fresh-guy image would last for Andreas.

The shop assistant came to help them.

The second Sunday of March was Carnival Sunday, and Andreas and Alexis both turned up at the taxi office in the morning, two hours in advance to make sure they secured a seat. The carnival procession was to start at noon, following the children's parade. The sun was out, but the air was chilly. Alexis had a slightly short, black, habit-style dress with a white bodice, starched white collar, black headdress with a white bandeau, netted black stockings, and a big black shoulder bag. She did not know if she would be allowed in the taxi, so she covered her legs with a knee-length jacket. She carried the glittering, black, almond-shaped mask in her pocket.

Andreas's ice cream cone costume was made from foam. The white ice cream shape had multicoloured dots over the head and chest. It had a hole for the face and, of course, for the licking tongue too. The cone structure went below his chest down to his knees. He rolled it up and placed it in a carrier bag.

He was going to tuck into it in Limassol and wear it over his black trousers and long-sleeved jumper due to uncertain weather. He settled into the front seat to the cheerful greetings of the passengers. It was carnival time! Alexis took a back seat, giving the impression of an innocent commuter. The taxi was now full and moved on, some singing carnival songs with the driver joining in at times.

It was a mild, sunny day in Limassol, but mingled with a danger of heavy rain pouring. Wind was blowing, and both Alexis and Andreas were worried about the possible downpour of rain. They got ready in their costumes to join the procession at the end that was reserved for individuals. Andreas placed his empty carrier bag into Alexis's shoulder bag, as he would need it to take his costume back in the taxi. They waited for their turn to join in. The procession began in full swing, with an audience lining the street on both sides for miles to watch the colourful pageant go by. Groups were parading, and some danced in vibrant troop costumes and coloured hairpieces. Tractors pulling carts displayed local produce and carried puppet faces. Musicians were on the sides of the road. Some were being towed in carts while playing music, both Greek and Western. Exuberant joy showed on everyone's faces. Alexis and Andreas joined in the dancing. Everyone was having a carefree and magnificent time, and it turned out as the priest had explained it to them. And, of course, Andreas did not need a lesson to wink at girls; he was a free, unattached man again.

Both Andreas and Alexis were dancing to the music. From behind her mask, she saw someone she knew! She nudged Andreas to look in the direction of the children excitedly pointing towards Andreas and cupping their mouths, giggling at the tempting ice cream cone with chunky legs in black trousers jutting out from the padded costume.

He was easily noticeable, as his face was not covered. Members of the Williams family from Nicosia were in the audience, but it did not look as though they had recognised Alexis yet. She quickly detached herself from Andreas and slowly made her way to the other side of the parade, away from where they were standing. She was just feeling safe from being embarrassed, but—oh no—she noticed another soul from her sociable society! It was the priest from the Troodos Mountains.

She was nestled in by the costume-clad crowd, between the Williamses on the left side and the priest on the right side. There was no running away this time. And the procession was not moving that fast either. She quickly realised that she was not going to be much farther away from the priest's cassock either. She inched backwards to join the middle section, but there was no space for her to squeeze in there. Then she heard a loud, anonymous voice.

"Look, there is a sexy nun in the procession!" A finger pointed at her.

She tried to hide. It would not have mattered if the priest she knew was not nearby, but he was, and she wanted to avoid his eyes. She kept on walking without looking in the direction of the priest. Keeping time with the music, she zoomed past him undetected. Her glittering mask did the job, and her rush of adrenaline subsided! The priest was unmoved by the nun's clothing, though. Alexis figured this was not the first time he had seen this in a parade, but what would have been his thoughts if he knew who was behind the catlike mask? He would have been taken aback!

Once she was a safe distance away from the priest, she looked back to scan for Andreas. He was busy shuffling along, conversing with a young couple who swung their arms as they held hands and took small dance steps, skipping to Greek music playing from the sideline. They were dressed in colourful, traditional Greek Cypriot costumes. The female wore a long red skirt and a headscarf, white blouse, and an outer embroidered black waistcoat. The male was in black, baggy knee-pants, *vrakas*, an embroidered red waistcoat, white shirt, knee-length boots, red waist sash, and tasselled cap.

Alexis sidestepped from the procession and asked a policeman to take photographs of her with her camera. She waited for Andreas on the sideline, and when he came by, she joined him in the procession again. He was relieved to have found her in such a large crowd. She asked the policeman to take more pictures of them, including the traditional Greek costumes of Andreas's new friends so she could show them to Sven. She rushed back to collect her camera from the cop, as she did not want this camera to go missing too, and thanked him. He found her nun costume amusing. Alexis was having great fun on her last fling of complete freedom in Cyprus before she left for Sweden.

It was getting dark and windy, and Alexis tapped Andreas's shoulders to inform him that it was getting late now. She put on her jacket. She told him that the parade would go on until nighttime, but they had to return, and there was the danger of a thunderstorm too. She reminded him that at this time of the year, it usually rained at night in the seaside towns. Andreas was like a bee to flowers as he moved among groups of women, and it did not look as if he wanted to return without a visit to the pub, so Alexis decided to return on her own. She asked him to give her his cone costume so she could take it with her. He did. She urged him to return home in the last night cab. She left in a shuttle taxi with the excess baggage.

Andreas returned in a taxi with a bunch of giggling foreign girls. They were all returning to Nicosia, and the taxi driver, who was in his sixties, kept himself quietly occupied amid the noise by munching pitted green olives from a container. It was windy, and the road was quiet. At one time, Andreas felt like pinching an olive from his tin and tossing it at the taxi driver's head, but sensibly he quickly realised that he would get thrown out, and it was difficult to get another taxi at this time of the day.

Andreas was sitting like King Carnival; in the backseat, he sat with three girls, and in the front sat a small girl who kept on turning back so as not to get left out of the fun and laughter. When they arrived in Nicosia, they asked to be dropped near their homes. It was easy for the taxi driver, as the girls lived in one area, all working for the hospitality trade.

The taxi driver remained occupied with eating his green olives, as he knew too that the calcium from it kept his bone structure strong; these olives would be an investment towards his future old-aged legs. He did not want to end up being pushed around in a wheelbarrow at the mercy of the handler in a joyous ride on a smooth road, his timeworn legs dangling in the air or bobbing up and down in the wheelbarrow like a bobbin on a shaky sewing machine.

On the following day, Monday, it hailed and thundered with heavy rain all day. Alexis had to go to work at the Odena Hotel, and she showed them the costume she had worn at the carnival, which she had to return to the shop. The old-fashioned maids were stunned and thought it was demeaning towards the nuns. Alexis found it all entertaining, but at the same time, she was glad that her Cypriot kinsfolk and the reputable people she knew had not seen her. After all, her relatives thought of her as a zany foreigner.

After some days, Andreas had a tale for Alexis. He had now become good friends with manicured Grandma Cordelia; she pioneered a meeting between Andreas and a young Armenian girl, Izabella. Her family were neighbours of Grandma Cordelia, and Izabella had come with her to the supermarket where Andreas worked. They were introduced and had become acquaintances. Andreas said about Izabella, "Fortunately, she is not Grandma Cordelia's daughter!" Both laughed out loud.

Chapter 18

Marriage Proposal—Is It an Acceptance or Refusal?

Sven was more settled towards marriage, whereas Alexis was toying with it. On his next visit, he conveyed this to her. She went quiet. Her problem was she had a fear of marriage: gamophobia. She was hiding behind career building. There was silence in the room.

Then, Alexis plucked up her courage and the volcano lava of gamophobia oozed out. She explained to him amid tears and heavings how she felt about marriage, but she *did* love him. She relayed her fears of commitment and divorce. It was now time for Sven to be taken aback. The best he could do was listen and comfort her and convince her that both marriage and career could go together.

Subsequently, Sven visited a jewellery shop in Ledra Street in the old city, and purchased two plain gold bands—these were engagement rings, one for Alexis and one for himself. There was no shortage of gold there. It was in plentiful supply, and prices were reasonable too. He got their names engraved on the inside of the band with the engagement date and the year, 1989. Following a Swedish tradition, Alexis would receive a band with

Sven's name on it and vice versa. Sven would wear the band with Alexis's name on it. They would "carry" each other wherever they went.

He completed the set by purchasing two gold bands: the wedding ring had a line of diamonds with a wedding date to be engraved on the inside at a later date, and another plain one for motherhood. In total, Alexis would wear three rings, if she agreed.

Then came the nerve-wracking moment; he was going to raise the marriage question to her. At Olynasa Pub, where they had sealed their friendship, he popped the question and asked her to marry him. Alexis, in a state of trembling and excitement, said, "Yes." Sven placed the engagement ring on her finger, and he wore his too, a plain gold band. The wedding was scheduled to take place in Sweden next year. Michael made the announcement in the pub, people clapped, and they toasted to a drink. Marsha, Michael's girlfriend, joined them later.

Another Twist in Their Fate

Then there was a twist in Sven and Alexis's plan in Sweden; there was a deviation to their arrangements.

In Cyprus, Alexis's grandparents held an engagement party for them in their village. Just at the right time, Alexis's parents came too from England. They saw a vast change in their daughter, a more responsible person. But Alexis still desired secretly to sneak off to go on her hitch-hiking sprees. They all danced, drank, and sang.

Towards the end, her strong-willed grandmother, small in stature, called Alexis aside and told her the devastating news. Her father was like a time bomb about to go off! He had type 1 diabetes, and to make it worse, he was overweight and smoked heavily, which made him very prone to stroke, heart disease, eye damage, and limb amputation. This was the reason why they were in Cyprus. It was to give him a healthier lifestyle, fresh air, and time to go for long walks. And if he had to die, then he would do so on familial soil.

He was trying to give up smoking and lessen the intake of alcohol, but with difficulty. He was surviving on insulin injections to make up for the lack of it. His wife insisted that he get a gastric band fitted upon the advice of the doctor, but he declined, as he was scared that he would not wake up from the operation. So, he was resorting to taking long walks around the village. This did him good, though, as he met people on the way who cheered him up.

Alexis called Sven and told him the regrettable news. Quietly, she wept some tears, and Sven comforted her. He ran his hand down her back and gave her his shoulder to cry on. Her mother joined them, and the grandmother did not beat around the bush. She gently asked them to get married there, before leaving for Sweden. They certainly could not refuse her. Sven and Alexis accepted.

A few days later, the wedding date was set. Arrangements began in haste. The village hall and church were booked; the nearest church was outside the village. Alexis's grandparents selected the priest. The choice was bound to make Alexis chuckle.

Alexis's and Sven's time in Cyprus was coming to an end. Sven gave notice to leave the army. As it was, he would not be allowed to continue working as a peacekeeping officer in Cyprus once he got married to Alexis, who had a Cypriot blood connection. As a peacekeeping officer, he had to be neutral, and this would affect this view. Alexis informed all her employers and her landlord that she was getting married and leaving for Sweden. It was around Easter.

When the wedding time got nearer, Alexis remembered Molly and that she would have been her bridesmaid; now, she was going to keep it simple without one. Alexis stopped working three weeks in advance, as she had the wedding arrangements to deal with and the packing to do. Sven had organised a cargo company to transport their belongings together.

She bid farewell to all her employers. During a farewell visit to Mrs. Williams, her former employer gave Alexis a report on their carnival trip. Mrs. Williams informed her of fun-loving Andreas being at the carnival. She gave Alexis the news that there had been a "girl" wearing a naughty nun's costume, and as she did, she lifted her eyebrows and widened her eyes! Alexis remained tight-lipped, and all she could do was laugh under her breath. At a time like this, she would have welcomed deafness!

The wedding was kept small. Both Sven's and the rest of Alexis's immediate family attended the wedding. Some of Alexis's family came from abroad. Alexis invited Michael, Marsha, and Andreas, and Sven invited two of his workmates, and one was his best man. But they forgot that the villagers were not going to be left out! They all turned up too, and those who could not get in gathered outside, clapping and cheering to see the bride and groom. Invitations did not need to be sent out!

Andreas was invited with his companion—this time, his painted tricycle cart with buntings! Andreas in his best black suit rode Alexis to the church in her white lacy wedding gown and a crown of myrtle leaves, a Swedish tradition. He blew the horn, and drivers on the road hooted back with people waving and children following. Alexis was in a state of numbness, not knowing how to feel or react.

While on their way to the church, disaster struck! One of the cart's wheels became loose. Andreas had cleaned the wheels, but he had forgotten to tighten the bolts.

Oh no. What to do? Alexis, with no time left to waste, followed her instinct —hitchhiking. And she stood on the side of the road and stuck her finger out. It did not take long before a cheerful couple in a dented car stopped for her. This was the same car she had collided with, a junker ready for the scrapyard, when she was riding her bicycle with a broken finger. She and the driver recognised each other. The student driver was awestruck, widening his eyes and rolling his eyeballs, as if he was face to face with a superstar who was doing a video shoot. Alexis muffled her laughter. She controlled her giggles and explained to them what had happened, and the lady happily helped her and hurled her into the back of the car, and the driver began to hoot. Alexis turned round from her seat to wave at Andreas, and he blew his horn back as he got to work on his wheel. Alexis's car hooted at intervals, and she got worried that the car battery would go flat. No, it did not. She reached the church half an hour late, and her father was seated at the door, waiting for her to be given away with her mother. She told her dad to ask questions later when he saw the dented car near the door and stammered, pointing towards it.

Sven was waiting at the door with her bouquet, a Greek tradition, and wondered anxiously what had happened. He was restless, shuffling from one foot to another. He stood in his wedding attire, a black suit, white shirt, and bow tie. He thought that perhaps the fright had taken over and she had backed off, and oh, yes, he was greatly relieved to see his snow-flake. This saved him from an embarrassment, as his family had travelled from Sweden. They had passed on a Swedish tradition to Alexis, usually reserved for the daughters, of wearing one silver coin in her left shoe, from her father-in-law, and one gold coin in her right, from her mother-in-law. This was to ensure that she would never go without money.

Alexis's parents gave her away to the groom. She took the bouquet, they both walked down the aisle, and she saw the priest. She stood still for a quick moment and giggled. He was the priest from Omodos, the one who had been at the carnival and had witnessed her in a nun's costume. She could not tell if he had recognised her, though.

The wedding ceremony was performed according to both Greek and Swedish traditions. Sven and Alexis went through the traditional ceremony with both sets of parents by their sides. The family members placed the marriage crowns on their heads with a ribbon binding the two crowns, normally done by the best man and bridesmaid. During the ceremony, the priest gave the couple ceremonial bread, *prosfora,* to eat, and both husband and wife drank red Cypriot wine from the same glass, representing the sharing of the cup of life and the biblical wedding, where water was turned into wine.

Andreas arrived panting and composed himself as Sven gave Alexis two gold bands: the diamond wedding ring with the date 3 June 1989 and both their names engraved on the inside, and another for motherhood.

The priest blessed them in prayer for a long and happy life together and removed the crowns. The newly wedded couple offered the guests sugared almonds to represent endurance and sweetness of marriage. As the pair left the church, the guests threw uncooked rice and flowers, for fertility and joy, and then Alexis tossed her bouquet at the unmarried girls. Marsha caught it, meaning she was the next to marry!

The church service was followed by a reception with abundant gaiety—Greek music, dancing, eating, and drinking at the village hall. Alexis's father took a glass of wine when his wife came over to remind him that only one glass was enough or an ambulance would have to be called. He obeyed and, while seated, bonded with the joyous mood, clapping his hands in time with the Greek songs. Andreas sprang into action too. He was not going to be left out and be a Humpty Dumpty who sat on the wall and ran away when the girls came out. Oh no, he joined in the dancing, jubilantly, and so did Michael and Marsha. Flowers were thrown at the bride and groom, a practice that had replaced the traditional plate throwing due to safety, and bank notes were pinned to the bride and groom's clothes as they danced, including Swedish currency from the Swedish family. This paid for their tickets to Sweden!

Stockholm was where they were heading. It was a city of fourteen islands connected with bridges, and each had its own unique character. It consisted of the Old Town (Gamla Stan) with narrow cobblestone streets, old buildings, and the Swedish Royal Palace, and the new, modern section with designer shops and government buildings. They would spend their honeymoon touring the beautiful islands.

They also planned for Christmas a short romantic break at the Icehotel in Swedish Lapland, the world's first hotel made completely of snow and ice, which melted in summer and was redesigned for December to April. This was a novelty for both, nestling up under reindeer hides and sleeping bags in the icy room, trying husky sledging, and viewing the northern lights—a spectacle of colourful dancing lights in the sky. They looked forward to this memorable stay.

Epilogue

Larnaca Airport

Sven and Alexis were all packed to go. Her final rent was paid, and the landlord was unemotional. He was used to bidding farewell to his tenants; according to him, there was always another in the pipeline.

A day before departure, Alexis went to say good-bye to her grandparents, who wished her well with shaking heads. They were wondering what heights she would trampoline to in Sweden. Alexis insisted her parents stay in the village due to her father's unexpected ailments, and she did not know if she would see him alive again. But she kept a cheerful front, as she did not want to add stress and cause a stroke. It was hard on Alexis to bid farewell to her family members, as well as Michael and Andreas, and she felt choked.

The day finally came for them to leave for the airport in Larnaca. The afternoon was windy with the sun shining mildly. On the way, they saw a billboard for the singer Alexis T. She was to perform around the island. Alexis pointed excitedly towards the billboard to make Sven aware of it.

"Look, she is in town. I had a brush with her on my first day in Cyprus as a student." Alexis giggled. "I will tell you about it later."

They arrived at the airport, checked in their luggage, and waited for the announcement for the flight departure. Alexis needed a dose of cheering, as she was feeling sad and hollow at leaving Cyprus. Ahead of them, they saw classy Grandma Cordelia and her jolly husband. They were the uplifting dose that had come to bid them farewell. She was dressed in a flowery jumper, and Grandpa Pierre wore rugged facial hair and a green jumper. The so-called designer stubble had become fashionable after the unshaven look in the popular American television show

169

Miami Vice, and Grandpa wanted to be a part of it too, as the busy bee that he was needed to keep buzzing.

Alexis gasped in happiness, and the atmosphere became chirpy and cheerful once again around them. Alexis introduced the elderly couple to Sven. He remembered Grandma Cordelia from the brief encounter he'd had with her at Olynasa Pub, when he had walked in with the flowers for Alexis. While the ladies were busy chatting, Sven and Grandpa Pierre disappeared from the scene for a sneaky treat. They returned with a bunch of flowers for Grandma Cordelia and a single red rose for Alexis. Both ladies were delighted.

"Oh, how wonderful, my dear," exclaimed Grandma Cordelia, and she leaned across to give her husband a kiss on his cheek. She also received an envelope from her husband. It was a pair of tickets to Alexis T.'s show. Alexis gave her clean-shaven Sven a peck too.

Grandma Cordelia's hands were full now; she had a sound, safe scheme to keep them occupied just in case she found out that her husband was meeting a Filipino girl on that particular day at Olynasa Pub. Alexis's hands were busy with hand luggage. She placed her rose into the corner gap of her handbag.

Alexis turned around and in a soft tone reminded Grandma of an event that had taken place when Grandma was walking down the road and she had pointed her trolley at the tricycle driver when he sounded the bugle at her.

"Do you know who that driver was in that colourful tricycle cart?"

Grandpa felt greatly relieved that he was not the only one with secrets.

"No, I don't," replied Grandma Cordelia in an anxious tone.

"It was Andreas," answered Alexis in a calm note. She did not want to upset her.

"Oh, was it him!" exclaimed Grandma. It took time to sink in. She felt a touch of embarrassment, but would Andreas now receive an apology or a scolding? And where better to patch things up with Andreas than at Olynasa Pub? But Grandpa Pierre had no plans to go there with his wife. Of course, he had a reason not to—he would have a brood of Venuses walking up to him!

The announcement for their departure came over the speakers. Alexis and Sven said their good-byes and began their long walk to the departure lounge. Alexis turned around, and, with mischief in her voice, she said to Grandma Cordelia, "Don't forget to enrol for javelin classes."

Grandpa Pierre's eyes sparkled with delight. He thought that was a great suggestion. He would use this opportunity to pop out for a glass of beer. Guess where? Of course, Olynasa Pub, but there was a certain danger of his wife walking in there with her javelin missile!

Sven Karlsson and his snowflake, Alexis Theodorou, boarded the plane. Grandma Cordelia and Grandpa Pierre watched from the airport balcony as they flew off. They returned home ruminating on their youthful days. At home, Grandma placed her bunch of flowers in a vase.

"Oh, how lovely they look," she affirmed.

Grandpa Pierre took off his shoes, stretched his legs onto a stool, and grabbed a bottle of Commandaria wine and a glass. He'd watch some television. He removed his dentures as an excuse to avoid talking to his wife, just in case she probed further into his discreet pub trails. Without teeth, all he could do was mumble; an edentulous person would find it difficult to clearly pronounce some letter sounds. His wife went to cook bean soup, a recipe of hers that he enjoyed. She later came and joined him in drinking wine, while he wolfed down his tasty soup.

Pierre wondered if the troubling questions would be coming now.

Grandma did not touch the topic of Olynasa Pub, but instead asked him in a relaxed and reflective tone if he still remembered what her father had said to him when he took the wedding vows. He grinned, gave a nod, and reminisced about the stern warning he had received on commitment. He smiled at the thought that his father-in-law had forgotten to advise him on how to fly the nest in old age! He finished his meal, and both toasted to Alexis and Sven's future. What better way than with Commandaria, which already had a romantic legend attached to it? They both looked forward to going to the concert of the singer Alexis T.

Sven and Alexis settled in their seats and contemplated their future together. *No more hitchhiking,* she pondered and smiled. Sven then went quiet as he gazed outside and reflected on his past army life. Alexis broke the silence. She cheered up the atmosphere with her story about the five-star hotel and her mistaken identity on her first day in Cyprus with the singer Alexis T.

A middle-aged man in the seat next to them across the aisle was reading a magazine that had Alexis T. on the front cover. It got their attention. They looked at each other and burst out laughing.

Sven then took out a small gift wrapped in a box in Easter paper and gave it to Alexis. She opened it, and it was a whistle! He had not forgotten to get one for himself either. He raised his to show her. "To stop the arguments," he announced.

The jubilant atmosphere exalted their moods as the plane took its elevated position in the sky. Alexis leaned her head on Sven's shoulder, and she smiled, reflecting on the receptionist at the booking office for the East Coast boat trip while they waited for the air hostess to bring some refreshments. She also thought of Molly, of what she would have done if the two of them had had an argument and the whistle had been blown. Molly would have stood there, showing her smiling, protruding white teeth at the receptionist to show that she was the innocent saint.

Alexis reflected on their married life together and she wished for the traditional Rhodian sweet, melekouni, to see what mischief it would play on them, as she pondered on her future. She thought of having a family, but she first wanted to adjust to living in Sweden, learning the language (although English was widely spoken), and establishing her work ambition. Her thoughts streamed to Sven, as he would have to find temporary work first.

Their lives together sparkled like the first gleam of dawn, shining brighter and brighter till the light of the day was in full and glorious sunlight.

I have glorified thee on the earth: I have
finished the work which thou gavest me to do.
John 14:4 (King James Version)

END

About the Author

Z Vally is neither a Cypriot nor a Turk, and has no political interest in Cyprus. But the author does have a strong familiarity with the area and a deep interest in writing about it. In the 1980s, Z lived in the Greek-speaking southern region of Cyprus, near the Green Line buffer zone, and traveled extensively around the region. These experiences and more have been cleverly woven into Z's debut title, *The Green Line Divide: Romance, Travel, and Turmoils*.

Now residing in the United Kingdom, Z previously studied finance and business at a British college, and enjoys sewing, cooking, baking, and do-it-yourself projects when not writing. The author also fancies residential architecture, landscape, sightseeing, reading newspapers, and watching TV news and documentaries.

40133406R00110

Made in the USA
Charleston, SC
25 March 2015